T0369435

Einstein's Lament

and other writings

by

Frederic deJavanne, Ph.D.

(An De Zhe 安德哲)

"I want to know all God's thoughts; the rest are details."

Albert Einstein

Order this book online at www.trafford.com
or email orders@trafford.com

Most Trafford titles are also available at major online book retailers.

Note for Librarians: A cataloguing record for this book is available from Library
and Archives Canada at www.collectionscanada.ca/amicus/index-e.html

Printed in Victoria, BC, Canada.

ISBN: 978-1-4251-7124-7 (soft)
ISBN: 978-1-4251-7125-4 (ebook)

 www.trafford.com

North America & international
toll-free: 1 888 232 4444 (USA & Canada)
phone: 250 383 6864 ♦ fax: 250 383 6804 ♦ email: info@trafford.com

The United Kingdom & Europe
phone: +44 (0)1865 487 395 ♦ local rate: 0845 230 9601
facsimile: +44 (0)1865 481 507 ♦ email: info.uk@trafford.com

Also by the author:

Books
Time Currents
Beware the Fury
Waterlogged Chopstix
Ulysses: The Comic Apocalypse
Spoken English for Chinese Speakers
Lazy English: Rose and Lily come to America
Word Power (English & Chinese)

Music CD's
Live at the Palace
The Phantom of the Piano

Anthology
Spiritual Modalities:
Religion, Tolerance and Freedom of Conscience

Dedicated to my colleague, mentor and friend, Darrell Moffitt, superb mathematician and physicist, Texas maverick, wild man of Los Alamos, who, instead of leading the sacred cows to the slaughter, mercifully put them out to pasture. Los Alamos will never be the same!

Table of Contents

"Never lose a holy curiosity."

Albert Einstein

INTRODUCTION

QUANTUM VS. CLASSICAL
THE REVOLUTION IN PHYSICS

Reality is merely an illusion, albeit a very persistent one.

Albert Einstein

<u>Shifting paradigms: strange underpinnings</u>

The 20th century witnessed two major departures from physics' Newtonian past: first Einstein's relativity, which he developed from 1905 through 1916, and the much more radical departure, quantum physics, which didn't fully emerge until the mid 1920's, a group effort which focused on the sub-atomic world and whose astounding and totally unexpected results turned physics upside down.

In 1900 quantum physics was quietly born. Max Planck served as the father *and* the midwife. Like all revolutionary scientific discoveries, it wasn't welcomed or even believed at first, was often ridiculed, generally ignored, or viewed as a mere anomaly. But in his study of "black bodies" (bodies that completely absorb radiant energy), one stubborn fact just wouldn't go away. Planck found that, contrary to what visual perspective and common sense tell us, energy *doesn't* flow smoothly and continuously like a river; instead, it's transmitted in tiny packets, which he called *quanta*. A scientist's scientist, Planck, who became a Nobel laureate, was able to calculate, with great precision, the ratio between the frequency of the emitting source of a quantum and its energy; this became the all-important "Planck's constant,"[1] one of the smallest in physics, indicative of the extremely small scale at which quantum events occur.

The seeds of the coming revolution in physics had begun to quicken with James Clerk Maxwell's "Treatise on Electricity and Magnetism" in 1873. Maxwell's equations describing electricity and magnetism proved that they were not discrete phenomena but one and the same — thus electromagnetism. This was a huge breakthrough portending major changes to come. Then there was the famous Michelson and Morley "ether wind" experiment (1887) to measure the speed of light under varying conditions, which proved, to their own dismay, that light doesn't behave like ordinary matter, but, in fact, appears to act independently — quite aloof from the motions, interactions and complex agglomerations of denser matter such as a fast moving train or a spinning planet--that it always "travels" at the same speed, no matter how much speed you add to or subtract from the emitting source — no

---

1   Planck's constant: 6.2606×10^{-34} Ratio between the *energy* of a photon (E), and its frequency (V).

matter what the "inertial reference frame"[2] of that source. The experiment actually failed in terms of the original intent of Michelson and Morley, but ended up turning classical physics on its head. All this occurred barely a decade before Planck's discoveries.

At the outset, few realized the stunning implications of what Max Planck had begun, but the horse was out of the barn. A lot of new questions were raised about what might *really* be going on in the sub-atomic realm, at the tiniest scales that could be inferred or imagined. The deeper they probed, the stranger it became. Many of the young Turks in the scientific world – both physicists and mathematicians -- began casting about for a theory that could take all this into account and still remain self-consistent, much to the discomfort of the old Classicists, some of them early Ayatollahs of Academe. The earth had begun to tremble.

In 1905, Einstein published his theory of special relativity[2], "The Electrodynamics of Moving Bodies." The implications of special relativity were far reaching and revolutionary: space and time, no longer conceivable as separate realms or discrete entities, were shown to be linked -- locked in the mysterious dance of dilation and compression, circumscribed and interpenetrated by Nature's seeming absolutes, the strange constants such as "c"—lightspeed in a vacuum. Henri Poincaré, a far greater mathematician than Einstein, was the one who had

---

2   Special principle of relativity: "If a system of coordinates K is chosen so that, in relation to it, physical laws hold good in their simplest form, the same laws hold good in relation to any other system of coordinates K' (K-prime) moving in uniform translation relatively to K.."

actually created the equations *and* noticed those radical implications five years earlier. But he simply could not bring himself to believe them.

Radically unorthodox as the theory of special relativity seemed, it remained arguably within the realm of Classical theory. At that early stage, quantum and classical had not yet parted ways. That would gradually happen over the next 25 years.

In 1915 Einstein published his theory of general relativity, which included the 20th century's most famous formula, setting forth the equivalence of mass and energy, **e=mc²**: the amount of energy (*e*) in a given quantity of mass (*m*) is calculated by multiplying by that quantity by a factor equal to the speed of light (*c*) multiplied by itself. Note that the number to be squared is not 186,000 (which is *miles* per second), but approximately 300,000,000 (which is *meters* per second). The exact speed of light in a vacuum is 299,792.457 meters per second, which multiplied by itself – squared – comes to just under $9*10^{16}$ --90,000,000,000,000,000 – a factor of nearly 90 quadrillion.

The seemingly abstract mathematics became a grim reality for the first time when the first A-bomb was set off in July, 1945 in the New Mexico desert – the birth of the atomic era. It was the very first real-world application of the formula. We all know the rest of the story, which became the true source of Einstein's lamentations.

Another proof of general relativity came with his theory that gravity could actually bend light waves – noticeably when they passed a massive object. The dramatic proof occurred in 1919 during a solar eclipse when bent starlight was actually detected *behind* the planet Mercury (not very far behind). Largely because of this, Einstein, in 1922, was awarded the Nobel Prize in physics for "services to theoretical physics, and especially his discovery of the law of the photoelectric effect", although the Nobel judges all knew that the prize was long overdue for him.

Einstein, early on, had acknowledged and confirmed that the photons – the light 'particles' or 'waves' – fit Planck's description of quanta. So, at the time – only a few years after Planck's discoveries -- it could have been argued that Einstein had leapt upon the quantum bandwagon, acknowledging that light was transmitted not in a smooth flow but in *quanta* – tiny, discrete 'lumps' or corpuscles -- adding to the slowly gathering momentum (pun not fully intended). But as time passed, second thoughts, bordering on alarm, would come as Einstein and his cohorts gradually became aware that our seemingly ordered physical reality (to say nothing of the mental) floats blithely upon an utterly capricious and unpredictable quantum sea, seemingly ruled by probabilities. Possibilities of the possible as possible.

Could the action of the experimenter – the 'observer effect' -- exert a direct bearing on the result? Indeed, *what are the physics of intent*, and the paths of *its* trajectories?[3]

---

3   And what are the physics of the undeniably electrical realities of visualization, of precise imaging in both the dream states and the waking states, indeed, of thought itself, and the application of thought in truly altering the physics of "real-world" states of affairs? Is this exclusively the realm of the pseudo-science, psychology, or still in the realm of philosophy? Or physics, as it ought to be? We eagerly await the advent of the 21st century Einstein's and Poincaré's who will discover the mathematics of these crucial questions. No T. O. E. (theory of everything) can claim validity and universality without answering these questions.

If an experimenter's willed action actually changed the results of the experiment, lending specific characteristics to a sub-atomic particle/wave as a result, or pulling it out of the quantum soup like a fish out of a pond –a revolutionary concept -- it would then appear that, by means of a conscious act, a probability "wave", representing a potential event, had been actualized, had been brought into manifest existence, *creating an event in real time.*

All this was disturbing news for Einstein, who had steadfastly maintained, "The **belief** in an external world independent of the perceiving subject is the basis of all natural science." [my italics]. For many practitioners of hard science this was a powerful *mantra* that expressed the very soul of modern science, implying an absolute duality between object and subject. Even for those who accepted it only provisionally, it continued to serve as a practical and wildly successful working model; few were willing to risk killing the goose that had laid so many golden scientific eggs, or embark on a wild goose chase[4], to further milk the metaphor. Few exhibited the inclination – or the patience – to question it and attempt to deal with the complex epistemological and ontological questions that would arise if the "external world" and perceiving subject were somehow related and interdependent -- questions with which, it must be acknowledged, Einstein constantly grappled with.

Each of us instinctively understands <u>space</u> as "objective," implying an external world, *out there*, as in "independent of the perceiving subject." We believe what

---

4   A Confucian proverb, by the way.

we see – 'seeing is believing.'[5] Conversely, we experience time as "subjective," *in here* (although in the larger view, all sensory processing is internal and therefore subjective at base). Therein, space relates to visualization and is processed, instinctively understood, "viewed", as external or objective. Time, on the other hand, is *felt*; it is tied naturally to internal perceptions in which sequentiality is implied, principally (though not exclusively) to sound, as in language and music.

Vision *binds space* simultaneously (as in viewing a painting): a static frame with a myriad of details which is instantly grasped as a whole. Hearing *binds time* sequentially (as, for example, in listening to a musical composition or to a conversation), as the conceptual wholes unfold piecemeal within our minds at varying rates, depending upon the context. Add *process*, sequentiality – time -- to a static *visual* image with its virtually infinite details, and it moves, comes alive. Add the sound and, *voilà*, within the living consciousness of each observer, you have a complex, comprehensible, transmissible, fully integrated live image, their intersection an ever driven, ever-moving cursor of the now, rolling on the world line it inscribes afresh upon the curvature of spacetime.

Seeing and hearing, within ourselves the natural cognates to time and space, are discrete human senses, emerging from a deeper, prior, proto-sensory level that

---

5   In Act I, Scene I of *Hamlet*, we witness Shakespeare, through the character, Horatio, speculating on the validity of the visual sense data, *affirming it* in Horatio's mind. Having seen the ghost of King Hamlet, Horatio, initially skeptical, says, "Before my God, I might not this believe without the sensible and true avouch of mine own eyes."

seethes and courses within our psyches like a molten river of living emotion. The two senses are intrinsically and powerfully grasped, synaesthetes notwithstanding, as distinct and different. If we reflect on them, replay them, our instinctive belief system tells us they are separate, dual, *ganz andere* (wholly other), and this was a belief even the great Poincaré could not give up – though the truth lay before his eyes in his own formulations. But the 26 year old Einstein, in a moment of supreme inspiration seldom equaled in the annals of human thought, made the leap, intuited the connection and unified them.

So why not a second giant leap -- into Quantum Country? For him, a second Copernican revolution, following hard upon the first, might have been simply beyond the pale.

Within the old *mantra*, of course, the key word is "belief", although "provisional belief" is the actual implication, since all experiments are designed -- by their very nature -- to *find out* actual states of affairs. "*If we knew what it was we were doing, it wouldn't be called research, would it?*" Einstein famously quipped.

Speculation and creative imagination in this kind of detective work are necessarily part of the process. Nobody knew this better than Einstein. But long entrenched convictions are not surrendered lightly -- even for him. In his own case, the seeming rule of probability, implying pure potentiality – the hegemony of probability at the subatomic level -- portended drastic revisions of his most basic axioms, which, short of demonstrable proof, he was unwilling to undertake. And in the minds of many of his classical colleagues, the quantum world was the devil's ante-room.

Bertrand Russell had something to say to *those* "true believers": "*What is needed is not the will to believe but the wish to find out.*"

Quantum Wars

Along came young Werner Heisenberg with the *uncertainty principle*, with proofs incontrovertible that position and momentum couldn't be simultaneously pinpointed.[6] His discovery of this immutable law came as a surprise, as much to Heisenberg himself as to the rest of the physics community, especially Einstein, who didn't like it and never truly accepted it. Even Niels Bohr, when Heisenberg first presented it to him, tried to attribute it to measurement error, to the crudity of the instruments. But it persisted. It seemed the last straw, the final outrage to the traditionalists. Little did they suspect that still greater surprises lay in wait.

By the mid-1920's Erwin Schrödinger's wave equations and his elegant picture of the atom with its shimmering electron field were at least comprehensible to the old school, a kind of bridge between the quantum and classical worlds, which Schrödinger, a syncretist at heart, had endeavored

---

6   In QM (quantum mechanics), position and velocity of particles have a *probability distribution*, not exact values. The narrower this probability distribution is made in ascertaining position, the wider it becomes in ascertaining momentum, and vice versa. The implications of this discovery painfully undermined some of QM's deepest assumptions,.and created the first "atomic war" between the major physicists of the day.

mightily to build. Some of the classicists grudgingly agreed and joined in, but the bridge was beginning to show structural flaws. Heisenberg's version offered no such consolation; it was pure symbol; it could not be visualized.

The two versions could not possibly co-exist; if one was right the other was wrong, plain and simple. Battle lines were clearly drawn and no compromises were possible. There would be triumphant victory and abject defeat. Taking those stakes into account, it's not surprising that the two men were now embroiled in a virtual blood feud. But Heisenberg was quickly gaining ground. He now had Neils Bohr on his side and enlisted the redoubtable Max Born to refine the mathematical foundation.

Quantum mechanics (QM) was about to make a quantum leap, from the old to the new, threatening to demote Schrödinger's version to the dubious honor of becoming an anachronism in QM's first "old school." One could fantasize what an atom might look like, but it quickly became clear that there was no scientific basis for visualizing its structure, none whatsoever. Gone were the elegance and the symmetry, replaced by pure abstraction – endless, wearisome sets of numbers.

Heisenberg and Bohr won this battle, Schrödinger lost, and QM had now entered Phase Two. And for the first time in his career, Einstein found himself on the sidelines in a major physics controversy, though he was far from ready to give up. His arch-rival, Bohr, of course, took the lion's share of the credit, but Heisenberg's star had risen to the firmament, and Born's brightened as well.

Einstein's dream of a coherent *ligature* tying together all events in the universe in a deterministic fashion now seemed impossible if this unwelcome development turned out to be true and correct. If probability, discontinuity and uncertainty underpinned the entire phenomenal universe, the idea of an unbroken ligature – a continuous thread -- was out the window. It indeed seemed that God was playing dice with the universe, or "playing peek-a-boo" as Alan Watts later suggested. To reach beyond this dilemma, Einstein even became interested in the "many worlds" theories, parallel universes which, summed over, would actualize every probability; so did Hawking.

The implications of this new Copernican revolution were mind-boggling and touched every aspect of the field. They were also crazy-making, counter-intuitive, and began to depict the outlines of a world – at the deepest and most basic level - that was stranger than any philosopher, theologian or science fiction author could yet come up with. To quote Winston Churchill (entirely out of context), it was "*a riddle, wrapped in a mystery, inside an enigma*".[7]

A new term was aptly coined: "quantum weirdness."

New physical and temporal dimensions began popping up, and the physicists engaged the best mathematicians -- Hilbert, von Neumann and many others -- to come up with formulas that could make sense of all this. "Physics is far too complicated for physicists," Hilbert had once quipped.[8]

---

7   Winston Churchill October 1, 1939, in a speech about Stalinist Russia: "I cannot forecast to you the action of Russia. It is a riddle, wrapped in a mystery, inside an enigma."
8   Princeton's Ed Witten, who today stands at the very front rank in both theoretical physics *and* mathematics, would have made Hilbert eat his words.

The plot thickened – or attenuated.

The controversy raged on; decades passed but no unified solutions presented themselves; the gap remained stubbornly unbridgeable -- if anything, growing wider. In 1935, the time period in which the epic poem, *Einstein's Lament*, is set, Einstein and two colleagues, Boris Podolsky and Nathan Rosen, convinced that unknown variables must be hidden in this morass, created a thought experiment (monogrammed "EPR")[9] to seek the proofs that these variables do indeed exist – or could at least be inferred. However, as with Michelson-Morley, the experiment didn't turn out as expected; it seemed to confirm what they were attempting to disprove.

Curiouser and curiouser – Bell's theorem -- physics to metaphysics

"Imagination is more important than knowledge. Knowledge is limited. Imagination encircles world. . . . The more I study physics, the more I am drawn to metaphysics." (*Einstein*)

The year was 1964 – perhaps not coincidentally the year that Peter Higgs, a Scotsman like Maxwell, brought forth the theory of the Higgs Boson. John Stewart Bell, an Irish schoolteacher like the great mathematical pioneer George Boole a century earlier, was the kind of professor we all loved – he endeavored with honesty, warmth and brilliance—and humor-- to make quantum theory

---

9   Einstein, Podolsky and Rosen (EPR): "Can quantum mechanical description of physical reality be considered complete?"

more understandable, to create, in his words, "a simple constructive model". Instead, he catapulted physics into an even weirder zone, but one which held out a promise for ultimate resolution – a clear window into deep reality.

This stunning discovery, coming only nine years after Einstein's death, was Professor Bell's *interconnectedness theorem* with its superluminal—faster than light—implications. "Any hidden-variable quantum theory must be non-local."[10] It proved that causal chains and pilot waves indeed "travel" faster than light, *instantaneously* in the minds of some – suggesting that time may not be a factor at all where interconnection – quantum entanglement -- exists. Bell's theorem also showed that, once two particles interact, a permanent and irreversible correlation (relationship) between them occurs, thus interconnectedness[11]. Considered by many prominent physicists to be the most important discovery of our age, requiring a drastic and dramatic revision of our concepts of space-time, Bell's theorem implies, at a radically fundamental level, that seemingly discrete events within our universe, even at distances comprising light years or light millennia, are connected—correlated, "entangled", in a most immediate and intimate manner.[12]

If Bell's theorem is correct, and every related experiment performed since has confirmed that it is, then the

---

10   Quote from John Stewart Bell

11   Or call them wavicles, probability waves, sub-atomic entities, whatever verbalism in appropriate context best serves to approximate the precise—and rather simple—mathematics that describe them.

12   Conservative physicists, however, believe this is "adding legs to the snake" (Chinese proverb), or "gilding the lily."

conclusion is unavoidable: either all the "parts" are *already* interconnected, *or* they're in the process of becoming so, progressively, ineluctably. To be sure, all arose from the "primordial atom" — their common mother, at the "Big Bang"[13] event, and were thus, in one way, related from the beginning. Having come into individual existence at various stages of the expansion process following the Big Bang, they began "finding" each other, reintegrating in a *cumulative* process –going on all over the universe. In this process, any and all compatible particle interactions, from the moment that they occur, unite the subject particles in an ascending series of trans-spatial and trans-temporal relationships, swelling inexorably towards a pristine moment when all the possibilities have been actualized – in factorial splendor – into an ultimate interconnectedness, an absolute saturation.

Either possibility fills the mind with wonder. And what will happen at the supreme moment when this total saturation is reached? Ponder this.

---

13   Or the latest Big Bang in an infinite series, known as the "bang, bang, bang...*n*" theory (which I personally favor, since it solves the "infinite regress" dilemma)..This, however, would require a series of "big crunches" (gnab gib), and the present accelerating expansion of the universe -- its conception fraught with unsubstantiated theories of dark matter and dark energy -- does not lend support to this idea. To thicken, or actually, to attenuate the plot, there are new speculations as to whether universal constants, such as "*c*", the speed of light, may change, may be tied to the expansion, and (possibly) to the contraction of the universe. *But* there may be another way of looking at creation, suggesting that new universes are coming into being all the time, from small to near-infinite scales within the mysterious singularities of black holes – from the super-massive ones at the centers of galaxies to smaller ones like Cygnus X-10 in our own neighborhood.

So is this science or science fiction? Science in new garb, it would appear, with certainties underpinned by -- bobbing on -- a foamy sea of non-actualized probabilities – of pure potentiality. The fact is that the "observer effect" consists not merely in the production of results arising from passive "observation" but implies action – directive action -- as well. One prominent Irish philosopher, George Berkeley, believed *perception* to underlie, and in a way, create our entire reality: *esse est percipi* – to be is to be perceived – by mind, though he had to explain why an object was still there after one stopped perceiving it, walked away, then returned to find it was still there.

But note also that Berkeley said *esse est percipi* --"to *be* perceived" and this is in the passive voice. With the "observer effect", it can take on characteristics of active voice, directive action – a transitive verb -- in nature. *Verb?* A mere word, you are thinking, just a part of speech. But the profound thinker and futurist, Buckminster Fuller, asked to define himself, promptly replied, "I am a verb."

It would thus appear that we sentient beings play an important role after all in the total picture, "the beknottedness of the plenum" as semanticist and philosopher Alfred Korzybski aptly characterized the living, oscillating universe, or, as Darrell Moffitt succinctly dubbed it, "the fizz."

Today, it is beginning to look as though the entire probability world, the sub-microscopic quantumworld, mediated on its boundary with the "normal" world by the huge, yet-to-be-confirmed Higgs boson (which fills the final gap in the Standard Model), springs through the Higgs, like Athena from the head of Zeus, fully armed into manifestation – "existence" -- by directed action of mind, human or otherwise: *will*, if you will.

In the series of experiments which began on September 10, 2008 (and were rudely interrupted a few days later), we eagerly await the results in CERN of the LHC – the large hardon collider – which is expected to reveal the "ghost in the machine" – the elusive Higgs boson, if, indeed, it exists. But keep in mind that *not* detecting it doesn't mean it doesn't exist. Do you smell a fault?

What about us?   The *anthropic principle*

Man is the measure of all things, oracled Socrates' teacher, Protagoras, nearly 2,500 years ago. This was and is the ultimate statement of the human equation, the "anthropic principle" --- that (pun fully intended) *mind matters.* Universal ideas -- conceptions of the very broadest scope-- were sought out and found by such truly modern thinkers of the ancient world. Those ideas dwelt within the domain of many of the great Greeks, who viewed the universe from the loftiest peaks of human thought - from the summit of philosophy. From this highest perspective arose the first T.O.E.'s – theories of everything -- in Western thought. Enter Anaxagoras, a skeptic of the first order and an older contemporary of Protagoras, with his own *quodlibet esse in quodlibet* – everything is in everything.

Their perspective bordered on the infinite.

Quantum physicists, at the opposite end of the scale, employing the most precise instrumentation devisable, were seeking the tiniest minutiae – exploring the subatomic realm – trying to puzzle out the dynamics that govern these strange entities and sub-, quasi- or proto- entities, if, indeed, they can be governed at all. Most avoided philosophy, preferring consciously to pursue their knowledge quest through ever more precise experimentation and statistical analysis.

Their perspective bordered on the infinitesimal.[14]

These modern men were ambushed by philosophy. The infinite has met the infinitesimal, the *uroboros* devours itself, *implicatio*[15], shrinking to a point, then uncoils itself, *explicatio*, into an expanding universe. In seeking *alpha* they encountered *omega*.

Protagoras, if alive today in Copenhagen, Vienna or Bern, might have modified his dictum to read "man is the measur*er* of all things." Then, discovering that the mere act of measuring changes things -- raising the ante still more -- they would discover another proof of the role of

---

14   Shakespeare, *Hamlet*, to Rosencrantz and Guildenstern: "I could be bounded in a nutshell and count myself a king of infinite space." William Blake: "To see the world in a grain of sand/ And a heaven in a wild flower, /Hold infinity in the palm of your hand /And eternity in an hour."
15   *Implicatio, explicatio*: Latin terms for *infolded (in-folding, coiling)* and *out-folding (unfolding, uncoiling)*. These terms were derived from the powerful metaphor, taken directly from nature, of the seed before germination – "implicatio", which contains all the genetic codes, and, after the key event of its germination, miraculously grows, unfolds, into a fully matured being in the physical world – "explicatio." The metaphor implies an intrinsic, living structural process, for the universal natural phenomena of contraction and expansion, infolding and outfolding of dimensions, and forms an integral part of Neo-Platonic philosophy from Plotinus (3rd century) to the present day.

the "observer effect" – of human mind being not merely that of passive observer but consciously active participator, human consciousness focused and directed, carrying out projects it has conceived on its own. One suspects that neither Protagoras nor Anaxagoras would have been as surprised as those 20th century physicists who, emerging from behind their rigid departmental confines, had their blinders rudely torn from their eyes.

So, could an act of will, man acting as *independent* variable, setting the values, arbitrarily add to the mix, make a real difference? We must never lose sight of the fact that the concept of independent variable, without which modern mathematics could not exist, necessarily implies a conscious operator who can change the values at will, following the dictates of his imagination. Man *is* the operator of the independent variable. His actions cross the boundary, and both sides change. The "observer effect" consists not merely in passive observation but in active participation, choices selected from a palette of possibilities, bringing about real events, tangible results in the manifested world. The results do not disappear, but, as with the "butterfly effect," cumulatively and permanently alter events that succeed them.

The Ayatollahs of Academe

Many of the mainstream scientists feared the murkiness, feared loss of control, in a domain they had dominated for more than a century; it smacked of theology and mysticism, which they still perceived as their mortal enemy. For over 300 years, since the founding of the Royal Society in 1660, the mainstream of science, advancing by leaps and bounds, had become increasingly – and more dogmatically -- skeptical, attempting to escape the tyranny of the churches and to divorce man from nature irrevocably. It allowed them gleefully to poke their fingers in the eyes of self-righteous theologians who ruled by authority, and who were, like all tyrants, loath to relinquish their power.

But as science usurped that authority in succeeding generations, politics entered the picture. The perennial human failing – the quest for power – rose to the fore once again as science supplanted the old theologies, and fundamentalism in new guise raised its ugly head, suppressing free and open inquiry, attempting to hold hostage the very soul of science. Many of these Ayatollahs of Academe initiated their own Inquisition, ruled with an iron hand and persecuted dissenters with as much zeal as their priestly forebears had done, resorting to ridicule and derision, ruining the reputations of honest researchers, denying professorships and tenure – their version of burning the heretics at the stake.

And few to this day have forgiven Isaac Newton – the most eminent scientist of the time and the most stubbornly persistent truth seeker – of daring to delve into the arcane realms.

But quantum physics itself was sounding more and more like theology. This drove the positivists and their ilk, the ayatollahs of science, to distraction. *Fear of chaos,* a mortal fear of being engulfed and swallowed up by The Blob[16], drove their wits still further astray. It terrified them.

"Man is a thinking reed," mused the great philosopher and mathematical pioneer, René Descartes, in the 17th century. How did man come about? As a "thinking reed", what is his nature, what are the laws of man's thought, his place in the universe? What is his relationship to his world, to realities and connections he could only imagine, even to those beyond Descartes' fertile imagination, beyond the end of his tether? To a god, answered Descartes, if such might exist; to *the* God, whom he claimed to have empirically "discovered" in his philosophical "reconstruction", adducing a series of rather stale medieval proofs for his existence.

Einstein expressed his belief in a god, "the Old One," quite simply and elegantly: "***The deep emotional conviction of the presence of a superior reasoning power, which is revealed in the incomprehensible universe, forms my idea of God.***" He wanted to know all His thoughts. He also acknowledged the anthropic principle and the necessity of incorporating it into any comprehensive theory. But it wasn't easy for him, because he still believed that the basis of all natural science implied "belief in an external

---

16   *The Blob*, a campy 1958 horror film, redone in 1988. A shapeless, slimy amoeba-like creature from outer space begins devouring humans by engulfing them and digesting them on the spot, and grows with each "meal" until it is the size of an office building, threatening to swallow up an entire town. In the 1988 domestic version, it is the result of a defense department experiment gone horribly wrong, with the same results: people are swallowed up by the shapeless chaotic, slimy creature, whose size and voracious appetite grow with each victim.

world independent of the perceiving subject" – a cold external universe to which humanity's joys and sorrows, dreams and aspirations – and experimentations -- seemed extraneous and irrelevant. But hope lay in the mysteries of the "observer effect" – in which our actions, our choices, made a difference after all.

And what of Einstein himself? If, indeed, we accept the premise that "a man can be no greater than the scope of his ambitions," the greatness achieved by this man, whose ambition was to know *all* God's thoughts, can be no surprise.

Frederic deJavanne (安德哲)
Harbin, China

PREFACE

Einstein the man

"If you want your children to be brilliant, teach them myths. If you want them to be very brilliant, teach them more myths."

Einstein belongs to all of us, is loved by all of us. In the public mind, he is a symbol of supreme intellectual power and achievement in the 20th century. Few have disagreed with Time Magazine's decision to name him "person of the century."

Born a German citizen; he became a citizen of Switzerland. Here his illustrious career as a theoretical physicist really began. He later returned to Germany in triumph as a Professor of Physics. He was born into a Jewish family (though he did not practice the formal rituals of Judaism), so people of Jewish origin worldwide, whether devout or secular, can claim him. Finally, in 1941, he became an American, which means that every American can take pride in his achievements. The worldwide scientific community proudly lays claim to him as well, though he was known, from time to time, to gently let the air out of the inflated egos of some of his colleagues. As with Abraham Lincoln, it can be said of Albert Einstein, "now he belongs to the ages."

"If my theory of relativity is proven successful, Germany will claim me as a German and France will declare that I am a citizen of the world. Should my theory prove untrue, France will say that I am a German and Germany will declare that I am a Jew."

He was very human, unshakably honest. To quote Prince Hamlet, describing his father, "he [above all] was a man." Einstein had the rare ability to laugh at himself, and in fact was often quite self-effacing. He also believed in "keeping it simple," although, he warned, "not too simple."

Religion and 20th century science

"Science without religion is lame; religion without science is blind."

Was Einstein an atheist, pitting science against religion? This was perhaps the unkindest cut of all, and it persisted for decades. For much of his life this bald faced lie was held up by fundamentalist Christians and even some hyper-orthodox Jews. Nothing could have been further from the truth. His belief in a god, whom he called *"the Old One"*, was strong and unwavering, though never rigid or dogmatic: *"My religion consists of a humble admiration of the illimitable superior spirit who reveals himself in the slight details we are able to perceive with our frail and feeble mind."* He often said that his whole endeavor was based on his need to know God's thoughts – *all* of them! He simply didn't believe in the formalities of religion, the rituals, the trappings, the need for human intervention in the spiritual lives of people. Many of these he found to be repugnant, believing that they bring out the worst in people. And, like the Buddhists, Einstein believed in the sanctity of all life.

But his faith in the human race was less enthusiastic: *"Only two things are infinite, the universe and human stupidity, and I'm not sure about the former."*

He also knew that traditional scientific method, working under the self-imposed limitations of the orthodox scientific world, could not easily explain the human condition. Was he a "positivist"? Far from it. He rejected the positivistic frame of thought because of the limitations it would impose upon the truth-seeking spirit of science, upon the free creative mind. Asked to comment on it, he replied, "It cannot give birth to anything living, only exterminate harmful vermin." Like Samuel Taylor Coleridge, Einstein believed in the supreme power of the imagination.

What about politics? When, a few years after the founding of the State of Israel, he was offered the presidency, he modestly but firmly declined. And government? *"The hardest thing in the world to understand is the income tax,"* he once quipped. A pointed message to the IRS, hopefully a lesson: if Einstein can't understand it, who can?!

Was Einstein ever wrong? To be sure! In his own words (perhaps being overly modest): *"I think and think for months and years. Ninety-nine times the conclusion is false. The hundredth time I am right."* Late in life he lamented that his greatest error was his theory of the "cosmological constant" (Λ, *lambda*) – an attempt to introduce a balancing factor that could account for the seeming stability in the universe, somewhat akin to Fred Hoyle's "steady state." He abandoned it when astronomer Edwin Hubble came up with the proofs that the universe was expanding. Now it turns out that he may have been in error about having been in error! The names have changed, but the cosmological constant *redivivus* has returned with a vengeance in several forms with theories concerning dark matter (and dark energy), zero-point energy, and numerous related theories to account for the accelerating galactic expansion.

So it seems Einstein was on the right path after all. To quote James Joyce (*Ulysses*), "A man of genius makes no mistakes. His errors are volitional and are the portals of discovery."

"Most of the fundamental ideas of science are essentially simple, and may, as a rule, be expressed in a language comprehensible to everyone." (Einstein)

James Joyce, who was in Zurich at the same time as Einstein (1919), said much the same thing about his own ideas, though his later writings -- *Ulysses* and *Finnegan's Wake* -- could scarcely be labeled as having been written "in a language comprehensible to everyone." Unfortunately, it appears that Joyce and Einstein never met. It would have been an historic meeting! There were many amazing parallels between their lives. *Time*, naming Einstein as "person of the century," named Joyce's *Ulysses*, "novel of the century."

Einstein, in the public mind, is a symbol of the pinnacle of intellectual power. Do you believe relativity to be some abstract, abstruse concept, far beyond the minds of us ordinary folk? It is not. And do you need a strong mathematical background to understand him? No again!

"Do not worry about your difficulties in mathematics; I assure you mine are still greater."

Much of the poem, *Einstein's Lament*, is about the human side of Einstein, his curiosity, his often quirky view of things, his humor, his humility, and his dogged persistence to find answers about what was really going on in the world around him.

"When you are courting a nice girl an hour seems like a second. When you sit on a red hot cinder a second seems like an hour. That's relativity."

"You ought to be able to explain relativity to a barmaid."

Above all shone his stubborn, scrupulous honesty. The saga of relativity in the 20th century is full of surprises, paradoxes, sardonic humor and salty characters – very human, like the man himself, who was ironical at times but never cynical, and who never lost his sense of humor:

"The only reason for time is so that everything doesn't happen at once."

TO THE READER

SYNOPSIS: ON READING
EINSTEIN'S LAMENT

This book is in three parts. Following the epic poem, *Einstein's Lament,* is a selection from my science fiction novel *Time Currents, Area 51*—about a Y2K accident that accidentally sends the entire base back to 1900, which the young Einstein becomes aware of. The final selection is another epic poem, "*Voyage of the Opal*"—the adventures of a twinned photon, a unit of consciousness, coursing through spacetime.

Do read the footnotes in both the poetry and prose selections, which are companion to the thoughts set forth in the text and actively dialogue with them. They are often irreverent, at times humorous, skeptical or even cynical, and often contradict the main texts, but they're also intended to help the reader by setting forth other viewpoints, furnishing factual information, dates and commentary about other scientists, mathematicians, world-changing experiments, philosophers ancient and modern, poets and dramatists. To quote Abraham Lincoln at some risk of redundancy, "explanations explanatory of things explained."

The first selection, *Einstein's Lament*, is the centerpiece of the book. Why the title "Einstein's Lament" *and what was he lamenting?* First and foremost, the most maddening dilemma of his life, whether he, a committed pacifist, should allow himself to sanction – and encourage -- President Roosevelt to develop the atom bomb lest Hitler's scientists, already working feverishly on it, develop it first, *or*, whether, true to his pacifist convictions, he should refuse to get involved. This is the man who, oxymoronically, said he would *fight* for peace. "If I were not a Jew, I would be a Quaker."

Einstein falls into a waking dream, resolved, come hell or high water, to find his way to God's abode, face him and ask him why, among other things, he seems to "play dice with the universe." In this lucid dream, "more real than real" he sets out on his journey-- and the adventures begin. He gets his wish -- the wish he had fondly nurtured from childhood – to ride on a beam of light, which becomes his carriage, his flying carpet, his magical transport through the saddle universe into the realms of light.

Einstein's Lament is my own speculation on what questions this great scientific pioneer might have asked the lords (and clowns) of the universe as to just what was going on, how, and why. Especially the quantum strangeness that seems to leave us at the mercy of chance – why God seemed determined (?!) to play dice with the universe.

If Einstein had actually made such a journey (and who can prove he didn't?), what would such a series of dialogues have been like? What questions, what answers? Once again, the currency is the world of ideas; Einstein asks questions, is confronted with a series of answers –not all of them consistent with one another. He is given sage advice on how to proceed with his journey, given directions and indirections, told what to expect, and, above all, to be prepared for the unexpected.

The second selection of the book (in prose) contains an excerpt from my novel *Time Currents, Area 51*, in which Einstein is a character. Time experiments, shrouded in mystery and secrecy, are being conducted in Area 51 on a very small scale. At midnight on December 31, 1999, a cataclysmic Y2K event has occurred, nearly starting World War III, then transporting everything and everybody at the base within a five mile spherical radius back to 1900, causing an instantaneous, multi-octave wave-event that reverberates through earth's energy field, to instruments and to minds -- a short-lived but powerful disruption of the space-time continuum. At first, nobody on the base knows that they're all back in 1900, because the base – at the five mile radius – is intact, self-sustaining, complete with backup generators. Not until they start to venture out into the surrounding countryside with jets and helicopters does the truth begin to dawn on them – they're back in 1900. Simultaneously with Nikola Tesla, Henri Poincaré, Jules Verne and others, the twenty year old Einstein becomes aware of this at the precise moment of the disruption, and his mind is set into furious motion.

The third selection is *Voyage of the Opal*, another epic poem – a frolic -- which presents the adventures of a twinned photon – a unit of consciousness. It courses through singularities, galaxies and Einstein's universe, accompanied by the would-be omniscient speaker in the poem, who during the journey, speculates on relativity, the true nature and meaning of space-time, reverse time travel, infinite velocity and many other scientific issues.

The "Theseus Approach"

When Theseus ventured into the labyrinth to confront the fearsome Minotaur, he trailed a thread behind him so he could find his way back to where he began. When I enter the labyrinth of a writer's mind, novelist, philosopher or poet, I try to enter into that mind *on the writer's terms*. I call this provisional acceptance the *Theseus approach*, after the Greek myth. First I take stock of my belief system, my orientation, at the beginning – taking note of where I stand at that moment. Then I can dive in with a fully open mind, lose myself if you will, involve myself fully in that person's ideas and perspective. At the end, I follow the thread back to my starting point and re-orient, allowing myself some time to digest them, and then feel free to incorporate whatever new ideas and insights I have learned during the journey, to revise my own views accordingly if appropriate.

In each of these three selections, you, the reader should bring to the table not only a vocabulary of terms, but also a *vocabulary of ideas*, and a strong dose of skepticism along with an open mind, and prepare to be challenged.

A human life – yours, mine or Einstein's -- is a cumulative work in progress, ever subject to revision, sometimes major revision. Skepticism is not only healthy, it is a survival mechanism for the inquiring mind and soul; it is a second wind for the Rat Race. A homeopathic dose of cynicism helps it as well; it allows for humor; it allows one to laugh at oneself. True science, as creative but disciplined truth- seeking, should be tinged with a salutary skepticism, giving the Imp that resides in all of us a bit of slack from its tight leash, looking around corners where nobody is supposed to look, actually having fun with it. But beware of allowing cynicism to take over, because, adopted as a self-indulgent philosophy of life, it is life-denying, an envenomed robe, a slow poison to the soul.

Use of the second person

Poems are spoken *directly* to you, the listener – person to person, mind to mind. We seem to write for ourselves, but we cannot write or think in a vacuum, the vacuum of space (even the quantum vacuum!). *First person* is too close -- lonely, isolated or egotistical, *third person* is distant, abstract, on the other side of the room, but *second person* is intimate – one on one – eye to eye: it addresses *you* in a true dialogue. Sprites leap off the page, magically preserved in the structure, twists and turns of the seemingly inert printed words *until this very moment* as they dance through your mind; they interact; they are alive. Poetry, as well as song -- poetry set to music -- is the medium for addressing *you*, the second person, you who are reading these words at this unique moment in real time.

All three selections are part of an ongoing adventure story whose ending is not known, which indeed may have no ending.

Enjoy!

I

Einstein's Lament

An epic poem

Einstein's Lament

I cannot imagine a God who rewards and punishes the objects of his creation, and is but a reflection of human frailty.

Albert Einstein

<u>Prologue</u>

Back in nineteen thirty-five,
Four famous physicists did thrive,
Scarcely able to agree.
Each believed he held the key.
Einstein was senior in the cast
Bohr and Schrödinger came next,
Youthful Heisenberg the last.

The burning mystery that vexed
These dedicated men of science
(Who should have formed a grand alliance)
Was quantum versus classical.[1]
Was Newton's ordered universe
Now at best a fascicle,

A mental construct, newly nursed,
Or maybe just a special case
In nature, wherein minds could base
Their limited conjectures?
*Meso*cosmic architecture:
Symmetrical external order,
Self-inscribed, but at the border,
Spirit thrust of Amadeus
Mirroring itself in chaos.

What to make of all of this?
Science at a crucial juncture,
Skeptics, cynics, set to puncture
Mammoth holes within the surge,
History hanging in the verge,
Great experiments abounding,
Aristotle notwithstanding;
The finest thinkers of the land
Were locked in combat hand to hand.

When Albert Einstein was a boy,
Algebra became his toy.
He loved the "unknown quantity."
A youthful Sherlock Holmes on fire,
He sought the culprit "**x**"'s lair from

Baskerville to London slum.
This veritable Moriarty
Had now become his chief priority.
And as he grew to be a man,
Light, the mystery uncanny,
Became his prime preoccupation,
His most creative speculation,
Anticipating what he might
Learn riding on a beam of light:
This was his deepest heart's desire.

Over a pint of old McSorley's,
Watching the bubbles rise and fizz,
He pondered Michelson's and Morley's[2]
Proof: when any beam of light is
Fired east to gain advantage
From the speed of earth's rotation,
Precisely at the selfsame instant
A beam's deflected south or north,
It fails to heed the added speed,
Simply cannot outstrip or best
The beam that's fired from seeming rest.

Incessant curiosity
Concerning light's velocity
And other unknown attributes
Wouldn't give his brain a rest.
He'd have to put it to the test.

He made a daring leap of mind,
Angled Occam's cutting edge
A notch beyond the maximum,
Breached the hardened outer rind,
Eureka! Found a hidden seam,
Richest vein of purest gold,
Veritable mother lode!
He grasped the hidden implications
Of Henri Poincaré's equations:
Dropped a term and realized
The space-time metric *is* the field;
Dynamical object *and* the context
Wherein dynamics are revealed.

In a contrapuntal dance,
Expansion and contraction of
Their perfect reciprocities
In zero-sum equivalencies,
Space and time became space-time,

A perfect two-fold turning of
Extension and duration.
These implications Poincaré,[3]
A pioneer of relativity, yet
Thinking space and time immutable,
As disparate entities, irrefutable,
Had, to his ultimate regret,
Declined to speculate upon.

Einstein's relativity
Fomented Classical transition;
He thought the quanta mere statistics,
Vastly overblown heuristics,
Dismissing unknown variables
Yet to be discovered --
Minor Planck[4] within the platform.
A classicist at heart was Albert.
He stuck to his determinism,[5] sure that
Local causation was coherent,
Sure that Nature, independent,[6]
Stood aloof, was not influenced
By the tinkering of technicians.
But quantum factors newly found
Now pointed to a deeper order,
Quite capricious, discontinuous,

Events devoid of ligature
Metamagical, or worse;
Evinced through probabilities, but
Quite impossible to pinpoint
Both position and momentum –
"One or the other, never both --
Damnable uncertainty!
Is this the final dénouement?
Does God play dice with universe!?
Impossible! I don't believe it! "
With every fiber of his being,
This man of deep, abiding faith
Recoiled from such absurdities.
The Old One, author of this order,
Wouldn't gamble it away!

Neils Bohr accepted quantum findings,
Led the Copenhagen way of
Dealing with the quantum data
Along with Heisenberg and Born.[7]
Idle speculations on their meaning
Weren't justified at all,
Agreed that they were underlying
All the macroscopic world, but
Didn't think it made a difference,

Save in the atomic structures.
Something of a pragmatist,
He wouldn't take it any further.
Analyzing such conundrums
Didn't suit his Danish fancy.

But Schrödinger was fascinated
With the burning questions raised
By all these novel revelations,
And like the famous ape in Hamlet,
Now set forth to try conclusions.

Erwin Schrödinger cast the dice:
Experiment designed to test
His new equations, sought to learn
Why Nature, forced to answer questions
Posed through a contrived device,
Gave a resounding Yes *and* No,
A red *and* green light, but no yellow,
Both *and* Neither often reckoned,
Much like Abbott and Costello's
"Who's on first and What's on second?"
His cat, "*Inscrutable*" by name, [8]
Passed on, yet stayed alive and well
(Unhappily, you couldn't tell,

For her expression stayed the same).
Such feline pomposity!
Wages of curiosity!

"A mystery lurks in this enigma,
Shrouded in a deep conundrum.
Scientists should ignore the stigma,
Be courageous, not be humdrum.
Was it Fortune, fickle dame,
Who put the classic laws to shame?
Is Hilbert space the explanation:
Trans-dimensional relations?
I'll have to call that mad Hungarian
John von Neumann [9]; he's the clarion
Within this land to formulize
The math for all these strange surprises."

Now Albert Einstein was unhappy
With the wild speculations [10]
Schrödinger's experiment
Had brought about. He felt compelled
To verify it on his own.
Boris Podolsky and young Nate Rosen
Were carefully by Einstein chosen
To prove that Schrödinger was wrong,

As they'd suspected all along.
Local space is self-contained;
Cause and effect must be preserved;
Entities such as photons cannot
Magically change their nature
Sans direct connection joining
Them in other interactions.
Phase entanglement's a cop-out;
Provide the evidence or drop out!
They'd find the proof once and for all
That causal chains or pilot waves
Cannot exceed the posted limit
Of the constant speed of light.

They fashioned the experiment,
They monogrammed it E P R, [11]
And hitched their wagon to a star.

Unhappily, they lost the day;
Instead of triumph sowed confusion.
Causes simply weren't sequential;
Timed events seemed inessential.
George Washington's old bed was slept in;
Random variables crept in.

Instantaneous causal chains
Cudgeled poor old Albert's brains.
Why should wavicles of light
Exceed their limit? If they're right,
Determinism's dead as ash,
Divine foreknowledge in the trash!

Late one cool October evening,
Setting down his violin
And lying back upon his couch,
He closed his eyes. The radio
Played softly now: Bartok's[12] quartet.
He merged with it; a secret spring
Unsealed itself within his mind,
Flowing in unaccustomed troughs
As palpably it moved his thoughts.

He fell into a trance that night
And stepped into a world of light.

FOOTNOTES: PROLOGUE

[1] This cosmic – and sometimes comic – epic battle of Quantum vs. Classical continues. The war is over, but the politics of the aftermath continue– with bitter behaviorists and pissed off positivists (quantum mechanics won the war and every last one of the battles).

[2] Michelson-Morley "aether wind" experiment – 1888: A blockbuster experiment measuring lightspeed under varied conditions (believe it or not, they could measure it *very* accurately even then). Fired through a beam splitter set at a 45° angle, one beam traveled on the East/West axis, parallel with earth's rotation, while the other was deflected at right angles to it on the North/South axis. If an "aether wind" existed, and was borne along with earth's rotation (at about 1,000 MPH) as they suspected, the forward beam, headed East, would have arrived at its equidistant goal under a microsecond--μ -- earlier than the sideways one (light travels 982'± per microsecond). But no difference was detected – a null result! Designed to prove the existence of the *aether* (call it a conductive matrix in the void), it *failed* in terms of the original intent of the experimenters, but ended up turning classical physics on its head!

[3] Jules Henri Poincaré, 1854-1912, dubbed the "last universalist" in mathematics. His solution to the *three body problem*, one of the Holy Grails of mathematics (like Fermat's last theorem), while not perfect, consisted of 9

simultaneous differential equations, and was considered so ingenious that the distinguished mathematician, Weierstrass, said "this work is of such importance that its publication will inaugurate a new era in the history of celestial mechanics." Also, Poincaré's formulation of "sensitive dependence on initial conditions" was a milestone in the development of chaos theory. There are still many who passionately maintain that Poincaré was the true discoverer of special relativity.

[4] Can't resist those quibbles! Max Planck is the guy who started the whole quantum revolution when he discovered that energy is transmitted in packets or *quanta*. Einstein agreed, in his 1905 paper on the photoelectric effect, that light particles were indeed quanta, striking atoms and knocking electrons out of their nuclei. The disagreement came much later with the radical .implications of quantum theory.

Planck's most famous quote: "A new scientific truth does not triumph by convincing its opponents and making them see the light, but rather because its opponents eventually die, and a new generation grows up that is familiar with it."

[5] Now: why was Einstein determined to maintain "determinism"? Did this make him a fatalist? Not really. His stubbornly rational mind simply insisted that for every effect there must be an antecedent cause, and that we ought to be able to coherently identify and trace those causes in both directions. In other words, he staunchly believed in a *ligature* or unbroken connection tying together all events in a given local system, even those at the tiniest scales. But this was precisely the point at which quantum physics and

classical physics parted ways, as he would later find out to his chagrin.

[6] This adds *true cosmic meaning* to the hackneyed cliché, "There goes the neighborhood!" Much of the impassioned controversy between Einstein and his quantum adversaries centered on the issue of neighboring or *local space*. Since he thought "c", light-speed, was the ultimate speed limit of light in a vacuum, he refused to go along with the idea of "action-at-a-distance" (except where gravity was concerned), reasoning "how could anyone possibly know, if the signal hadn't got there yet?" – a monstrous absurdity to Einstein.

[7] We regard quantum mechanics as a complete theory for which the fundamental physical and mathematical hypotheses are no longer susceptible to modification." *Werner Heisenberg and Max Born, 1927.*

[8] A well-meaning British matron called the SPCA (*Society for the Prevention of Cruelty to Animals*), reading that Schrödinger's poor cat, victimized in this cruel experiment, was both dead *and* alive. In this experiment (a thought experiment only), there was a 50% chance that a wave would trip a switch (which would shatter a vial, release cyanide gas and kill the cat), and a 50% chance that it would miss, leaving it alive. Since the experimenters' participation could change the result, the box containing the cat would never be opened, so the operation of pure probability was left uninterfered with. Thus, since the result was unknowable but the probabilities even; the imaginary cat could be said to be both alive and dead.

[9] John Von Neumann: arguably the 20th century's greatest mathematician (some would nominate Ramanujan for that honor). Another candidate, David Hilbert (q.v.), who flourished a few decades earlier, was no slouch either, though he was a heavy partyer and loved the ladies (far more scandalous in those days!). Hilbert also invented a pitching machine for pro baseball. One of his more notable quotes was: "Physics is far too complicated to be left to the physicists!" Add Poincaré to this list as well although much of his pioneering work was done in the 19th century (he died in 1912).

[10] After spending a lifetime attempting with great care to isolate and prove certain truths about the universe, many scientists found themselves driven to exasperation when these wild speculations captured the popular imagination with a vengeance. Their wits were driven still further astray by the capriciousness, discontinuity and craziness of the quantum world. Einstein, Hawking and others took some comfort in the "many worlds" interpretation, which seemed to offer the only resolution of the paradoxes inherent within quantum theory

[11] EPR: Einstein/Podolsky/Rosen. "Can Quantum-Mechanical Description of Physical Reality Be Considered Complete?" The EPR experiment, much to Einstein's chagrin, appeared to indicate that causal chains and/or pilot waves were reaching the goal before they should -- instantaneously -- or at least at speeds far exceeding "c", the speed of light. In hockey terms, the goalie knew way too much: he knew when the puck was on its way and knew its precise path *before* it arrived (ironically, like Cassandra, he could prophesy but couldn't do anything about it

[except place a lightning fast bet on the outcome!]). If the puck was traveling at the speed of light, then the advance warning *had* to be moving faster – or instantaneously. This drove many semi- or neo-classical physicists, including Einstein, to distraction.

[12] Bela Bartok's String Quartet # 5 (1934), known to synaesthetes as an intense musical source of the play of colors in the mind, exceeded only by his posthumously (somewhat controversially) edited 2nd Viola Concerto. Bartok, pioneering Hungarian-Jewish composer, escaped the Nazis and spent his last years in New York, sponsored by some of our own greatest musicians including the legendary conductor Serge Koussevitzky. There, until his untimely death, he composed prolifically, atonally and brilliantly. Einstein was known to dislike 20th century (mainly atonal) music, but is said to have made an exception in Bartok's case.

First Canto

God gave me the stubbornness of a mule, and a fairly keen scent.

Albert Einstein

<u>The Dweller on the Threshold</u>

As Albert Einstein's craft took flight,
He leapt astride a beam of light.
On photon boulevards astraddle,
A standing wave would be his saddle
(That is, if waves can really stand
Within the realm of light-speed land).
He stepped into a lucid dream
More real than real. He spied a beam
Of radiant celestial light
On the horizon, waxing bright.

To highest heaven he wished to fly
To ask the dread Creator why
He seemed to fling his dice awry.

Now present dangers seized his mind;
Floating in limbo, flying blind,
Like a moth, flew towards the glow,
In fear and wonder watched it grow.

Would it become a gentle landing,
Peace that passeth understanding?
Or would the life upon that plain
Be fraught with searing, blinding pain?
He didn't know and didn't care.
Come hell or heaven, he would dare.

Suddenly the craft was captured
In a gravitation field,
Accelerating rapidly
In free fall towards an unknown mass
Which gradually revealed details:
Earthlike, feral, dark, forbidding.
Sounds rose like an exhalation,
And heat; the air was thicker now,
And tinged with wisps of acrid smoke.
Below, the sea. A tempest raged,
Battering the craggy cliffs
With fury unrelenting. Now dark,
But darkness strangely visible;

Palpable shadows seemed to move
Upon the mountains, in the valleys.

As he drew near a darksome strain
Reverberated in his brain,
Grew louder and more ominous,
Though it remained anonymous,
Intoning notes eponymous
From gardens of Hieronymous.[1]

"Tis prudent here to lend an ear,"
The scientist echoed in his mind,
"For I am lacking clear directions."
Spirit and body weren't aligned,
He bent his will, he trained his ear
Upon the low and dark inflections.
At once the thundering words came clear:

"Gross bodies cannot roam at large.
The atmosphere is supercharged,
The frequencies at such a pitch
(Due constancy of Mr. Planck),[2]
Your brains would boil, your eyes pop out,
The moment that you entered in it;
You'd only have yourself to thank.

You wouldn't last a New York minute!
Like mortal maid in Zeus's den,
You'd fry 'ere you could count to ten.
So let's get something straight, my friend:
You're going to have to learn to parse
Your subtle body from your arse,
And there abide before you wend
Your way into the deep sanctorum,
Sanctum sanctorum angelorum."

The voice grew softer, droning on.
The atmosphere changed suddenly;
The sun burst through the thick cloud cover,
Scattering rays as through a prism.
Mists departed, cooler breezes
Wafted through the evergreens
That lined the mountains row on row.

"You're not the first to travel hither.
Remember Dante Alighieri,
Who had a pure and chaste ideal,
Of Jesus and the Virgin Mary,
Had lovely Beatrice in his creel
When he went angling for knowledge
In the exalted, sacred college.

That fellow had his head on straight
For separating church and state.
Like young Bill Ockham and Marsilius
And the peerless John Duns, *filius,*[3]
A plan had he to save the world
From base extremes of red or black,[4]
With sweet revenge on frauds and phonies,
And welcome respite for his cronies.
In choice Italian he unfurled
The subtle images impressed
Upon his deep, emulsive soul.
A yeoman's task, he did his best,
In telling of delight and dole,
A gift to his ungrateful world."

The speaker paused while Einstein's craft
Through lofty peaks and valleys flew.
But once again the sky grew dark;
Banks of fog and fitful winds
Revealed, bedimmed, a rocky seacoast
Far below, while thunder boomed
And lightning flashed. Wind-driven vertical
Sheets of rain obscured the view
As windowpanes ice-covered thinly,
But ceased abruptly as he landed.

He found himself upon a strand.
The fog dispersed; he stood before
The cave from which the voice poured forth,
Sat down upon a rock-hewn ledge
And took his bearings, gazed within.

The Dweller's face in part emerged,
Moving in and out of focus.
T'was huge, filled half the visual field.
Scowling, staring, enigmatic,
Now whimsical, now serious,
He bid a shallow welcome, then
Began to take his guest to task.

"But what is it you'd bring, my friend?
Ends to justify the means?
Means to justify the end?
What you call limning out of truth
Is based upon a specious premise,
A gross exuberance of youth
Extended into middle age,
As if you could exceed your tether,
Stand aloof, respect no person!
Hearken here a prime directive:
Know that your optimum perspective

(If you're to be the best detective)
Peaks in knowing what's objective
Attainable only in degree.
Ultimately a judgment call."

Suddenly he realized
That he had overstepped his bounds.
Demurred to Einstein, spoke more gently.
"My deep apologies, dear sir;
Sometimes I can't restrain myself.
This isolation drives me mad –
Years since I've heard a human voice.
It was not my intention to
Affront your dignity, your purpose;
We've serious matters to talk over."

The scientist nodded, watched the face
Grow smaller, down to normal size,
Retreating back into the dimness
Of the cave. The voice continued,
Softer now, and even-toned.

"Your mind is unencumbered now,
Your thoughts intact, accessible,
Expandable, transmutable,
Not regulated by the pulse,
Beyond the body's prison mesh
And the fleeting wisps of dreams.
Your consciousness is free of limits
Save those that you impose yourself!
Tabula rasa it must be --
Clean slate -- devoid of preconception,
If you're to glean the purest essence,
Divine embedding and imprinting
Of the truths to be revealed.

Subsisting in the borderlands
Upon the quantum boundary,
Its natural home, its true domain,
Mind derives its potent symbols,
From quantum side, *potentia,*
Mediated at the boundary,
Fertile womb of thought creation,
Nature's rarest essence, locked
With Spirit in perpetual union,
Obedient to your willed commands
Swiftly and unerringly,
Conforming to them perfectly.

'Tis limited but by the scope
Of your creative imaginings.
Infinitely accessible,
Malleable, subservient,
They manifest within your center,
Their natural home, where seeds of thought
Are germinated, form therein --
A perfect template, sensitive
In each detail of thought-creation.

A narrow border this is not,
Not limited by what you call 'real.'
Within its *virtual* dimensions,
Whose physics are yet undiscovered,
Mind can erect upon a whim,
A veritable universe
Of limitless expanse and scope,
Creatio ex nihilo,
Much like your Creator, parent flame
Of holy fire writ large that burns
Within your breast concordantly.
Independent variable 'tis,
Choices emanating from your will,
Logos-like dominating power,
From *you,* the conscious operator

Setting up your grand equations,
You who sets the power flowing,
Trips the switch and starts the music.

Portion of the grand design,
In universal order, prior,
In rank and in degree, still higher,
It cannot be selectively
Ignored or brushed aside.
Give mind its due, let it assume
Its proper place within the order.

Flame within the parent flame,
Your soul, full human, full divine's
Ensconced here in its primal power,
Your will, within its royal court,
Holds forth, issues its dread commands.

This ligature, the one you've sought
Exists, connects with God's own thought
As one with all of humankind
Within its *virtual* space, your mind,
Subsisting in unique dimension,
Controls duration and extension,
A stage where living dramas, schemes,
Nightly are performed as dreams.

You the playwright and director,
You creator and created,
You the players, you their thoughts,
You the subject and the object,
You the figure and the ground.
You the scenery, the air,
You the mind's eye, you the center.

With your daylight consciousness, your
Shared collective world, they play
As thoughts, imaginings and theories,
Analyses and syntheses,
Logic, ratiocination,
Plans, designs, technologies,
Language, symbols, and psychologies
At every order of abstraction --
Knowledge that's transmissible to
Other consciousnesses, thus
Binding time as well as space
In your collective waking world --
Civilization as you know it.
All that's human quickens there.

You've speculated on this matter,
Know it as Imagination,
But haven't found sufficient grounds
To take it further into science.
Beloved Newton, master of all,
Sought truth wherever he might find it,
Took his searches to the limit
Into venues preternormal,
Off the beaten track in regions
Scientists still fear to tread.
Made apologies to no one,
Found no warrant to delimit
Either the range or the domain.

So let your consciousness unfocus
In this divine collective locus.
Within the plenum, *boundless inscape,*
Source of all of our perceptions,
Paradox and paradigm--
The subtle mind of the divine,
Universe actual and potential,
Greater than which can't be conceived.[5]

Finite but unbounded, 'tis,
As well, a bound infinity.
Behold the new antinomy![6]

Seek your truths in *all* degrees
With diligence and competence.
And as you ride upon these beams,
Highway of super-consciousness,
The term, *illumination* will
Assume its truest, deepest meaning.
Pure thought must follow now in order.
All the data in, your mind must
Center full within itself,
Where focus and intensity
Of Will and of imagination
Burn off the impurities,
Forge in the white hot crucible
The purest gold of newest thought.

But now another term's been added,
Bringing new and present perils,
Science in her darkest hour,
Hanging Swords of Damocles
Above the heads of all of these.

As pacifist you spoke out boldly
For the deepest obligation
Of your colleagues to be wary
Of the deadly dangers of
Misusing scientific knowledge.
At the peak of your profession
Now you sit, but soon you'll learn
That from that higher vantage point,
You've risen to collective power,
Within a rarefied domain.
Here the politicians reach
For power and control of all.

More than scientist are you now!
The consequences of your actions
Loom far greater than before;
They touch the very heart of life
Upon your planet. So beware!
Ensconced with you within that tower,
Surveying all your precious planet
Lurks a raving madman poised
To utterly destroy your world.
Who will stay his bloody hand?
Who sits in that tower with him?
An *ivory* tower it is not;

The bridge for Spaceship Earth it is,
To paraphrase your friend Buckminster.[7]

The captain's chair's unoccupied, while
Chamberlain, Roosevelt and Hitler
Circle round the ship's controls;
The latter holds the best advantage.
Meanwhile, Churchill, rising fast,
Awaits his opportunity,
While Stalin, Mao Tse-Tung and Truman
Wait within the wings to join.

Reconsider now the error:
If old Pandora's box they open,
Free the genie, loose the terror,
Mankind's lot is dread and woe.
The enemy delves a yard below,
Plotting destruction of your kind,
Unreconciled twixt soul and mind.

The time must come when you'll consent,
Against your conscience, 'gainst your will,
To loosing a more horrid hent." [8]

"This cannot be," the scientist swore;
"Peace is precious, peace, not war!⁹
We just been through the war to end
All wars. Let science save the world!"

"Your pride's expansion, boldened now
By daring ratiocinations;
Your mind's most subtle penetrations
Obscure infolded crucial points,
Ensconced within subjective being
Turn your vision inward now,
Find hidden doors and passageways;
Own the deep totality
That is the essence of your soul.
You've not yet realized your power!
Spirit with intrinsic knowledge
Knows the universe is one.

Others there are, as you well know,
And well you know of whom I speak,
Whose search for knowledge self-corrupts.
'Tis arduous for that human mind
Clinging to its preconceptions,
Not originally built for theory,
Which, ever humbled in the struggle

Of the mind with grainy nature,
Looks for alternate rewards,
Seeks renown among his fellows,
Curries favor with the powers,
Casts about with baleful eye
Less to learn than justify,
Gathers up his meager winnings,
Fashions them like Galatea,[10]
Fabricates their underpinnings,
Calls them living and authentic.
These present the greatest danger."

Skeptically he listened as
His host unfolded all the horrors
Of another world war,
The pogroms and the holocaust,
And of the splitting of the atom.
Finally he turned to him,
Lamented, "I'm an academic,
Just a scientist, but one man
Who singlehandedly cannot
Reverse the tides of history!
In self-engrossed futility,
Cuchulain raged against the sea;
Marcellus cast his partisan

Against the woundless Danish air;
Quixote fought the fabled windmills."[11]

He gazed towards his interrogator
Shrouded in the deepest shadow,
And suddenly he grew suspicious.
"You sound like Mephistopheles
To Faustus[12] offering the keys
To knowledge, to philosophies.
Show your face, reveal your game,
Who are you really, what's your name?!"

The dweller's face loomed into view,
Smiling enigmatically.
"What does it matter who I am?
You've not done all your homework, man.
My name's a secret, my affair,
But if you'll come into my lair,
I'll have more secret knowledge for you,
And promise it will never Bohr you."

"By heaven, I charge, reveal yourself!
I know a half truth when I hear it.
I'll go no further; never fear it!"

"If you insist," the voice, now weaker,
Piped forth, "You are a great truth seeker.
You've fame already, seek no pelf.
You're on to me, OK, OK.
My job is not unlike Sir Kay,[13]
A *seneschal,* a jagged shard,
Castellan, yeoman of the guard,
Commissioned here to test the mettle
Of anyone who should approach
The inner sanctum of the tower.

Fodder for the moon I've been,
Misled thousands on their journey
Who sought my guidance earnestly.
My punishment is fitting, here to
Linger in this purgatory,
Help new seekers on their way
'Til arrogance, vainglory, bluster,
Deep ensconced within my being,
All are burnt and purged away.
Still fastened to my earthly frame, I am,
Detached, split off, 'til Saturn's round
Comes opposite in fourteen years.
I hold a purpose less than splendid.
I'm not allowed to pass within

Those gates by seraphim defended
Until my earthly body dies.

A sentinel I'm appointed here,
The guardian of a special light
Which penetrates the darkest corners,
Annihilates the deepest shadows,
First of four within a series,
For those who seek His sanctuary.
And if they're not prepared, they know,
And instantly they turn to go.
But since *you* seek with feet firm planted,
Your truths, and will submit to reason,
More knowledge you'll acquire in season.

Rewards are yours, your wish is granted,
And more's the merit in your bounty
For courageous pioneering.
Sloth and pride have not conspired
To contaminate your findings.
You've shunned the quick and easy path,
Traveled rough and thorny ground,
Stayed the course of honest seeking,
Sought the flaw within your being.

Move on my friend, my mission's ended;
More's to come, of nobler venue,
Richer fare upon your menu.
Ponder well my sage reminders;
Pursue your excellent adventure.
You've come most highly recommended.

And as to who *I* am, don't cower.
I answer to a lower power."

FOOTNOTES: FIRST CANTO

[1] Hieronymous Bosch's triptych, "The Garden of Earthly Delights" (1500 AD), a late medieval tragi-comic vision of hell-on-earth, hell-as-earth, or earth as hell.

[2] Planck's Constant – "h": A fixed ratio between frequency and energy: the higher the frequency, the greater the energy and vice-versa. Major building block in the world of quantum mechanics, and directly relatable to Heisenberg's uncertainty principle.

[3] Early 14th century philosophers, contemporaries of Dante, all of whom worked tirelessly towards the goal of the complete separation of church and state (cf. Dante's *De Monarchia)*. The French emperor, Philip the Fair, had, in 1303, marched on Rome and humiliated the power-hungry Pope Boniface VIII (who died shortly thereafter), and what was left of the papacy, now utterly devoid of secular power, was now moved to Avignon, France, where it remained for 80 years. Among these eminent philosophers were counted William of Ockham ("Occam's razor"), Marsilius of Padua *(Defender of the Peace)* and that fiercest of all scholastics, Duns Scotus (not to be confused with the seminal 9th century Neo-platonist, John Scotus Erigena).[1]   [1]Paradoxically, "dunce", a name bestowed upon the later Scotus's fanatical followers, came from the "Duns" in this 14th century Duns Scotus (and "Scotus" simply means Irishman).

[4] Red: the secular (also, the Army); Black, the ecclesiastical. State vs. Church, which, by the way, had just ended in favor of State (q.v. footnote 3). In Stendahl's early 19th century best seller, *The Red and the Black*, "red" refers specifically to secular arm – the army, and "black", of course, to the venerable Holy Roman Catholic and Apostolic Church

[5] Have a look at the structure of Anselm's Ontological Argument – an ancient exercise in self-transcendence, in which you mentally *continue* to conceive a series of beings/states-of-affairs *greater than, and inclusive of,* the one immediately prior. When you have reached the grandest conception, "greater than which cannot be conceived, " something magical can happen, because you have reached the mind's limit. The concept may rise from your mind, or off the page, to engulf book, reader and world. This was used by St. Anselm as a proof for the existence of God. The precocious Bertrand Russell, at age 19, proclaimed, "the ontological argument is sound!" but later reconsidered.

[6] Antinomy: read Immanuel Kant. Antinomies are opposing but equal concepts on a high order of abstraction, both of which can be proved, and, conversely, both of which can be disproved. Example: God exists vs. god does not exist.

[7] Bucky Fuller, seminal thinker, designer, architect and futurist, rumored to have had discussions with Einstein at Princeton.

[8] "Horrid hent": Hamlet is about to kill the king (Claudius) in the midst of his prayers, but decides that to do so in "the purging of his soul," would send him to heaven – be "higher in salary, not revenge." Urged on by

his father's ghost, he wants to destroy Claudius's soul as well as his body by killing him when he is in the midst of an act "that has no salvation in it." "Up sword," he says; it will soon find a more "horrid hent" in killing Uncle Claude. See also the McKenzie Bros. film *Strange Brew*, which is based on the plot of Hamlet.

[9] In 1955, Einstein and Bertrand Russell, both committed pacifists, wrote the following warning in the "Einstein-Russell Manifesto" and I quote: "Here, then is the problem which we present to you, stark and dreadful and inescapable. Shall we put an end to the human race, or shall mankind renounce war? . . . There lies before us, if we choose, continual progress in happiness, knowledge, and wisdom. Shall we, instead, choose death, because we cannot forget our quarrels? We appeal as human beings to human beings. Remember your humanity, and forget the rest. If you can do so, the way lies open to a new Paradise; if you cannot, there lies before you the risk of universal death."

[10] Do you remember George Bernard Shaw's *Pygmalion,* later adapted into the musical *My Fair Lady?* This came from the Greek myth *Pygmalion and Galatea.* Pygmalion was a skilled sculptor who fashioned a statue of a beautiful woman to such perfection that she came alive. He fell in love with his creation, Galatea (but she may not have fully returned the compliment)

[11] Classic literary figures from Irish legend, Shakespeare's Hamlet, and Don Quixote. The legendary Irish warrior Cuchulain (koo-HOO-lan), in his madness and war rage, waded into the ocean to do battle with the waves. For more about Cuchulain read *The Tain,* a compilation of

Irish legend. W.B. Yeats also writes passionately about Cuchulain. In *Hamlet*, at the very beginning, King Hamlet's ghost appears, and the soldier Marcellus throws his spear at him (to no avail). Incidentally, in Kenneth Branagh's unabridged *Hamlet* you'll see Jack Lemmon playing Marcellus (in one of his very last roles). *Don Quixote* you already know about.

[12] See Goethe's *Faust* and the series of temptations that Mephistopholes places before the protagonist, Dr. Faustus in attempting to snare his soul.

[13] Sir Kay, the Seneschal, mentioned in many of the medieval Arthurian romances, was the ill-tempered chief of the palace guard in King Arthur's court, assigned to limit access to His Royal Personage – not unlike H. R. Haldemann in the Nixon White House. "Every President has to have an SOB," he quipped, "and I'm Nixon's." Haldemann was Nixon's *seneschal*.

Second Canto

"To heed . . . that Power which erring men call Chance. . ."

John Milton

The Poets' Garden

He climbed upon the standing wave
And in a clockwise climbing turn
Accelerating near the limit,
Escaped the shadowy confines,
Looked back and viewed the caverns dim
Enshrouded in a back-lit mist
He found that he could see as well
From greater distances or nearer;
He needed only turn his mind,
Focus on the scene at hand,
And it would snap in consonance
To utter clarity. He beamed.

The light now brightened. Looking down,
Approaching from a dizzying height,
He spied a veritable Eden
Ringed by mountains, valleys, streams
Hidden in chiaroscuro.
Fleeting sunlight, scudding clouds,
Wind and rain from all directions
Whirled round in vortices
At speeds unnatural, like a dream,
Above the green elysium
Whose glowing, happy colors overwhelmed
The unadapted inner eye.

He flew towards it, slowed the craft
And marveled as the time slowed, too
(It wasn't s'posed to be that way).
He saw a huge gazebo there
Atop a gently rolling sward.
In the center, as on a throne
In Puritan garb a giant shape;
Auburn curls hung to his shoulders,
A fleshy face, enormous head,
Dark penetrating eyes, deep chin.[1]
This gardener smiled as he watched
The craft land deftly on the lawn.

"Welcome, my friend, please call me John.
I've much looked forward to your coming.
Sit you down and we shall talk
About your world, how it was born –
A world which rides upon a thought
As you have ridden on those beams."

He smiled and greeted his new host,
Inhaled the lilac perfumed air
And mounted the gazebo stairs.

The scientist looked hard into
Those deep-set piercing eyes. He spoke:
"But if the substrate of our order,
Quantum chaos, pure caprice,
Underpins and thus defines it,
How could it have come about?"

"The explanation I will offer
Abounds in metaphors divine
Such as *logos*, will and such.
Listen yet patiently and know
That seekers like you, in ancient times,
Did sound the depths of world and soul,
And were vouchsafed the truths they sought
In language they could understand.

Freedom's splendors scarce acknowledged --
Consciousness in novel feature,
Order as you understand it,
Rose from chaos' deepest roots
From our grandmother, Old Night,
Featureless for timeless eons,
Nothingness, *yet not privation*,
Instead, a generative void.
With the Father's dread command
At once sprang forth our mother, Nature,
Fecund womb, still fallow land,
Chaos held yet in potential.

Master lever activated,
Wondrous worlds unmanifest,
In one divine, defining moment,
Received the logos' single seed.
Point infinitesimal,
Infinite intensity,
First in number, sire of time,
Burst forth in splendor and in glory
In the hallowed, sacred ground.
Raised to order and duration,
It formed and grew the sacred bloom.
For logos, like your photon twinned,

Remains a singularity—
The bridge 'twixt time and timelessness—
Looking back at his creator,
Looking forward into nature,
A Janus[2] in the primal portal,
Joining unit and collective
Mystically in a dyad,
All existence His descendants,
Flames within the parent flame.
All revert to unitary
Life in their collective phase;
All disperse in deepest nature,
To the monad, to each point
Astride the flowing world lines,
Along space-time's continuum.

These structures pre-exist, it's true,
Enfolded in obscure dimensions,
(Remember that it's in *your* court!);
Those energies are yours and mine,
Each to his own, and fully felt,
And in dimensional orientation
Such as we live in, in our worlds.
We travel ever up and down
Those exponentiated gyres,

And feel the living energies,
Exult and suffer in their fires."

He listened, bore a wary eye,
His skepticism full aroused,
Yet half believed in terms provisional,
And let the ancient thoughts take hold,
Knowing they once had been original.
He sought a true Rosetta stone
Providing keys to unify
The complex and disparate world.
It filled his heart with hope and joy.

His deep ambitions thus comprised,
A goal he'd ever fantasized,
For nature's deepest secrets prized,
Knowledge enormous, power assized:
From deep obscurity he'd wrest,
Beyond the pearl of greatest price,
For science, the Mecca and Medina,
A pilgrimage of flame and hoar
To penetrate the world's deep core!
A warning voice, this time his own
Reminded him of Goethe's Faust,
And of his last interrogator.

A fine line must be sore maintained
And regularly re-examined;
Control such fantasies and keep
His keen scent on the trail of truth,
Remembering his prime directive.

He fixed his eyes upon the poet
And in the dim periphery
Saw other masters on the sward.

The Allegorist now stepped forth,
Bowing gently, took his hand,
Smiled and said "I, too, am John.[3]
I bid you welcome to our garden.

The understanding that you seek
Must draw from all the aspects of
Your total self, from mind and spirit,
From enlightened exercise of
Will, your greatest faculty,
Of power *esemplastic*,[4] of your
Imaging and imagining --
And of your moral judgments, weighing
Consequences on a scale.

Here deadly sins, *personified*,
Reverse in order, first with *lust*,[5]
And its companion, *gluttony*,
Imprisoning the pilgrim soul
Through enchantment and enticement
Enough to block the liberation
From the jealous body's sway.
Avarice, for pelf or knowledge
Renders up its secret longings,
Which the chela[6] cannot hide from.
Sloth consists of saboteurs,
Exiles with their own agendas,
Shadow figures, broken off,
Banished from the banquet table,
Holding energies in bondage,
Sapping the vitality.
Deep mistrust, unfounded fear of
Failure and humiliation,
Undeservedness, self-loathing,
Trap the will in tangled skeins.
Next is *anger*, ire unbridled:
From impatience and frustration,
Hotly born, fire of resentment,
Bursting forth like a volcano.
Envy cannot brook exposure,

Bear analogies invidious;
To the mirrored self, it's hideous.
Pride infects all generations
In pneumatic self-inflation,
Fills the spaces with itself,
Crowding out its boon companions,
Overweens the proper balance,
Arrogantly swells, and loudly
Flaunts its stilts and motley proudly."

"Thank you for your moral lecture.
Please allow me one conjecture.
Are these animated figures living?
Marching in a pilgrim's progress?
Sullen mates bound to my voyage,
Mutinous, morose and surly?"

"Yes, they live; they're separate beings.
No, they wish to be your friend,
For you're the key to their advancement.
These elementals, *bardo*-bound, are
Beings in-between the worlds,
Drawn from nature's hexagon of
Devas, jealous gods, hell-beings,
Beasts and hungry ghosts, *and* men.

Within their karmic circling bound,
They're species in samsaric round,[7]
Hoping someday to be free,
Ever yearning for promotion
To humanity's arena,
Ultimately Buddha nature.
They're beings yet of pure emotion,
Bound to you, and bound to nature,
Cobbled with your precious being,
Partly you and part their own.
They're driven by an urgent need
To bring to fore their inner light,
Which is contrary to the shadow
Nature that they manifest.
Needing balanced supervision,
They seek your stern and loving guidance.
T'were well that you should pay them heed."

"*Peregrin* am I, no doubt,"
The scientist mused to his new host,
"Who would become a *comprehensor*,[8]
Struggling to hold my course in
Navigating nature's ocean,
Winds and waves both port and starboard
Buffeting my fragile vessel.

If true these mates are my companions,
Not my thralls, I'll treat them kindly,
Be a stern but loving father,
Treat them as my fellow minions,
Feed them wholesome food, rewarding
Honest work and healthy balance,
With some playful recreation,
Helping them to nourish well
Those contraries within their being,
The virtues, ready to spring forth.
'Tis well upon an arduous voyage
To have companions, not be lonely.
For this much thanks!"

"The honor's mine."

"Sorry I'm so singleminded.
Gluttony, lust. are in the balance,
Both refer to appetition.
I've eaten countless birds and sheep;
A debt to each I owe, no doubt.
Through my peninsular appendage,
I've been a good disseminator,
A loyal soldier to the cause,
Enjoyed the sweetness and surrender,

Unmatched delights, caresses tender.
For knowledge, *avarice* I confess,
But my passion for the truth
Transcends this weakness, I surmise.
Sloth has never been an issue;
I concentrate for months on end
Until the barriers give way.
Anger doesn't burn so hot, though
Woolly thinking galls my kibe,
And fools I do not suffer lightly.
Envy? Well, I guess I'm lucky;
I'm at the summit of my game.
Pride's a vice I do project;
High standards I prefer to call it,
Integrity of intellect,
Although I'm always on my guard
Against the Faustian pride of mind.
Stricter with myself than others,
I've taken on a heady task.
A self-commissioned super-sleuth,
Seeks veiled and enigmatic truths,
Which, brought to light, are simple, basic
Concepts that a child can learn.

And on *that* point, may I inquire:
Why can't we talk in meters higher
Than dull iambs, singsong tetrameters,[9]
Thoughts encased in small diameters?"

"Because to discourse it is suited.
Terse, efficient declarations
Best are in these rhythms rooted.
But when you pass the final station,
Reach the zenith of your climb,
You'll hearken meters more sublime.
Meanwhile, you'll have a big surprise
Awaiting you at your next stop.
You'll have the answer to your question,
Provided you can re-examine
Many of your favorite notions."

Smiled the two poets, "Prepare yourself
For visions you have not imagined.
Laughter is the best defense
Whene'er your world turns raving mad!"

He smiled and bid his hosts adieu
"Haply have I stood this test.
My purpose holds as firm as ever."

The craft, on automatic pilot,
Rose again above the garden.
He tipped its wings, as both the poets
Waved goodbye from the gazebo,
Disappeared into the clouds,
Decelerated down to lightspeed
In a sea of timeless spaces,
Viewed the scene from all directions.

Implicate within a sphere,
Emerged a crystal polyhedron,
Rainbow glints within its facets.
Looming above it stood a palace
In garish, neon day-glo hues;
Glowing forth in ten dimensions.

FOOTNOTES: SECOND CANTO

¹ It's John Milton (in case you haven't figured it out). After Milton, it is said, only Shakespeare. After Shakespeare, only God. Read *Paradise Lost* one more time and follow the arguments closely. You'll find them to be amazingly modern.

² Janus: Early Greek god, perhaps the oldest of all, with two faces, one looking forward, one looking behind.

³ None other than that master of allegory, John Bunyan (a close contemporary of Milton), author of *Pilgrim's Progress*. Bunyan, who, more a prose writer than a poet, wrote but 72 poems in his life.

⁴ The term "esemplastic power", from Samuel Taylor Coleridge, one of the co-founders of the Romantic movement in English literature (with William Wordsworth), and one of the subtlest intellects of the 19ᵗʰ century. He implied that *imagination* is the human mind's truest creative force.

⁵ The Seven Deadly Sins, personified, italicized, and presented in reverse order. Would you have believed that *lust* was the very least of these?

⁶ *Chela*: a seeker, a dedicated student of spirituality attached to a *guru*.

⁷ Taken from the *Tibetan Book of the Dead* – a 8th century sacred book of Tibetan Buddhism written by the Savior of Tibet, Padma Sambhava. "Nature's hexagon....", etc. – a sacred geometrical figure, describes the six *lokas* or worlds of *samsara* —around and through which all souls must cycle until all attachments are surrendered and they attain enlightenment – i.e., Buddhahood. The *bardo* is the transitional state between physical death and rebirth through which all beings must pass.

⁸ *Peregrin* (a pilgrim) and *comprehensor* (one who has learned and understood) are terms used by the 14th century philosopher, Thomas Aquinas, to describe the state of the newly embodied human soul (*peregrin*) setting forth on the perilous seas of life, and its state upon successful completion of the journey (*comprehensor*).

Third Canto

The Player

*Not only does god play dice, but . . . he sometimes
throws them where they cannot be seen.*
                                        Stephen Hawking

Into the courtyard, Al, undaunted,
    Flew to seek the Ancient Gent.
On golden rays he pitched his tent.
Bright angels stood with flaming swords
    In ten directions round the Lord.
To his surprise, he wasn't challenged,
Dismounted from the standing wave;
    In a momentary stasis.
He sat him down and looked around.

And now the archetypal symbols
    Underwent a transformation,
All-perceiving synaesthetic[1]
    Integration of the senses,
Some he didn't know he had.

Chaos--ordered anti-pattern--
Flooded into his sensorium.
He saw a Mandelbrot mandala --
Kaleidoscope of strange attractors
Composed of exponential factors,
Phantasms from the brain of Esscher.
There sat a grinning cat, the Cheshire,
Frozen in death, but yet alive;
There Schrödinger and Heisenberg,
Lewis Carroll and C. S. Lewis[2]
(One was dead and three were living)
In Narnian splendor danced a jig.
While Erwin tooted his cornet,
And Heisenberg, perplexed, looked round,
Clive Lewis Carroll, a duet,
Piped plaintive strains of Louie Louie;[3]
On seeing Einstein, gave a start:
"Welcome, Albert, come take part!
Open your eyes, you're one third blind!
Not left or right, the middle one,
The one you didn't know was there."

He nodded, smiled, waved at them,
Opened chakra number six.[4]
Still intact in subtle body,

At once he saw in four dimensions,
Saw the Director's sense of humor.
The subatomic world leapt forth
In more dimensions, he liked it better.
All the particles were living
Entities, like playful children,
Yet unsupervised, spontaneous.
They danced and played and gamboled there;
They merged, appeared and disappeared:
For each, unique identity
In singlet state, or photon twinned,
Or of a hundred other classes,
Integrate, yet discontinuous.

Fascinated, yet obdurate, he
Tried to shut the Agni eye; [5]
Albert focused on his mission;
He soon regained his vaunted purpose.
"Perhaps we'll now bring back the aether,
Desperate measure though it be,
To try to save determinism.
If this, our deep reality,
Depends on these emergent flashes,
How can there be consistency
In laws of gross, dependent nature?

Causation links events in chain;
There *must* be ligature throughout,
Without the gross absurdities
Of happenings in stranger venues,
Unattainable in spacetime
If limited to the speed of light -,
A transgalactic butterfly
Effect[6] without coherent cause -
Ubiquity of influence
Attenuating all causation,
Still affecting distant loci.

If heavenly father holds the reins,
Perhaps he's *choosing* not to use them,
Perhaps to humor or amuse us.
But how can ordered universes
Sail on this strange, substrated sea,
Evinced through probabilities,
Without predictability?

Classic heaven or quantum hell?
He shut three eyes; he could not tell.
He'd plead his case; he'd be the scourge
Of woolly thinking quantum drones,
Report them to the demiurge.[6]
A sword of logic he would wield!

But curiosity overcame him.
The place was unfamiliar, yet
He had to see, opened all three.
He reeled aback, thought he was tripping.
The walls were glowing, rods and cones,
With strange attractors, fire and ice.
It looked disturbingly like Reno;
He found himself in a casino,
Addressed himself unto the Player
Perched astride a huge cloud chamber,
Casting dice of polyhedra.[7]

"Stop!" he cried unto the Deus,
"We'll all be overwhelmed by chaos.
I thought you were an engineer
Creating order far and near."

The Gambler answered while he threw
His dice into a murky dew.
"Since action at a distance thrives
And causal chains are instantaneous,
My dread commands ubiquitous,
Are celebratory, not iniquitous.
The ligature is in the chains,
And not within the gross events,

Which are *results*, not causes, see?
These causal chains invisible
Link to My will and thus to yours,
Which echoes Mine in microcosm—
Quite free to choose within its range--
Divinity that shapes your ends.
Those chains leave traces in the aether[8]
(*Quintessence,* if you like, *fifth element*),
Sarcophagi or moving tales,[9]
A psychic aether if you will,
Extensions of your present moment
Your race has shrunk down to a point
Of isolation self-imposed
In hyperfocus to insure
Survival in your bumpy world,
Scattering higher frequencies.

Limiting organ of the mind,
The brain is mired in language games,
Creating self-enclosèd worlds
Mistaken for totality.
Up here you must refine your focus
Center on the living present.
Focus, as threads drawn to a point,
Then, relax your focus tight;

Let the point become a blur;
It will clear up soon enough.

What you've perceived as past and future
Now will merge together in
A deeper and more spacious present.
Let it grow until your mind's eye
Can't quite see it all at once.
Orient within the circle;
See it then become a pristine
Sphere with poles, much like your world.
North is future, south is past,
Axis fixed whereon you travel.
Look now round the east and west:
See the axes of potential,
Spread out like a grand equator,
Ring of pure and endless light.

Here's the circuitry you seek;
Here the living energy:
Center now your will with Mine,
And feel the radii extend
To every niche of living mind.
Meaning of meaning there resides.

Divine events are miscellaneous
And local space just doesn't *matter*
The quibble stands, the pun's intentional,
Where local space remains conventional."

"Paradise or pair of dice?
I'll just remain a safe observer,
Immune to all that quantum fervor,
Aloof from my experiment,
Not misconstrued of my intent
To safely map out Nature's rules,
Retain the lattices of Boole.[10]
I'll *not* unjustly be accused
Of adding random variables
Just through my own participation
In circumspect experiments.
There must be other explanations.

And just what kind of a uni-verse,
Multi- or infini-verse,
Fashions order out of chaos,
Builds upon a house of cards,
Can make creation more obedient,
Make the human mind expedient,
Particularly mine." he parried.
You promised us a world!"

The Being smiled patiently as He spoke.
"This world's My *leela,* it's My play –
Ludic or just recreational.
You're a character within it;
I'm a lenient director.
Choose your method, learn your lines,
Improvise them if you wish,
Play your role just as you like it!"

"A world of classical parameters,
Where *pi* determines true diameters,
Irrational as it may be,[11]
That's just the world I want for me!
It's like the Wild West, so lawless;
How can the universe be flawless?
There's no speed limit in the land,
And two and two don't equal four,
It's anarchy! I'll take my stand,
And plead for justice, Neils Bohr --
Who buries his head in shifting sand
And what he doesn't see, ignores!
Occam's blade[12] has lost its edge
And you just perch there on the hedge!

I'll have none of it. There! If
You will just appoint me sheriff,
I will clean up this wild expanse,
Arrest those quantum miscreants,
And lock them in a narrow cell
To serve as their own private hell
The quantum pit in which they've fallen,
Which they keep trying to drag us all in."

"Enough !" the dread Creator cried,
"You're sounding like a holy roller,
A scientific ayatollah.
Awake from your dogmatic slumber!
You've come this far, so just stick to it!
Fainter hearts cannot break through it.
You must be bolder here, not humbler.
You've nearly got the magic number!
Form all the theories you have wrought,
A slight adjustment in the thought
Is all you need! Invert it! Not
Continuous spherical fields in spacetime
But spherical waves in continuous space.

A tiny element of thought
In terms of data you have brought,
Wriggling fishes you have caught
Will bring to light what you have sought
Unless you're just too overwrought,
Afraid you'll bring it all to naught.
You can't rule by authority;
The universe is just too free!"

"But there's the principle anthropic,[13]
Which holds in arctic clime or tropic,
Moral law that lies within,
Crowds of stars beheld in wonder.
Why is this paragon of beings,
Pinnacle of your creation,
Lacking so in your perfections,
Steeped in chaos, lies and blunder?"

"I tried to make a perfect species
(Though Jung had dreamt it but my feces);[14]
I only made one tiny error,
An engineering compromise,
On the insistence of my bride,
Your mother, Nature (I'm your sire).
And if you think I've sent a black doom,

Wait'll you see my quantum vacuum,
And meet those zippy nuts who stole[15]
The thunder from the blackest hole.

But I digress: one tiny error
Has made your kind a holy terror;
It's not my fault, one small effect,
Effect defective, a *de*fect:
I made your brain and made your penis,
(Your Elvis has a brother Enis)
You cannot use them both in tandem,
Desire to choose your mates at random;
It's just a minor disconnect.

Economy of circulation
Brooks no ratiocination.

A simple problem: when your focus
Concentrates within that locus,
Beware! Your conscience, still small voice,
Completely swamped by flumes of passion,
Virtually disconnects;
That command came from your mother.
Ontogeny, phylogeny,[16]
All she wants is progeny!

You're a loyal mother's son, too.
Membrum rigide; a rabbit,
Conscientiam non habet.[17]

Because you strove most valiantly
To seed all femininity,
There's merit in your bounty, Al.
For every brain and gleal cell
I wired within your bounteous brain,
We both endowed you equally
With genes and chromosomes to sow
Of peerless quality as well,
An equity which all should know
Instilled a grand imperative.
Your mother should be very proud!
Receive the gifts. You're in my debt.
Your god is not a prude, you know;
He even has a sense of humor.

Seeds cast in a fertile ground
Are for a time in matter bound.
Royal road to incarnation,
This is my best manifestation.

And now if you will please excuse me,
Dice are waiting. I must cast them.
Go now to your next appointment."

Albert left the gambling tables,
Closed three eyes in trepidation.

Space and time and Al were hurled
To the still point of the turning world,
Through *omphalos*, the world's navel,
Ensconced within the Great Attractor—[18]
Locus of the grand redactor—
Moment prior to all duration,
Moment ever evanescent,
Single moment opalescent,
Edge of multiplicity.
Beyond, a glowing crevice beckoned,
Light and dark's event horizon,
Toning forth a dread orison.
Eons seemed to pass. Apace,
He found himself in sacred space.

FOOTNOTES: THIRD CANTO

[1] Synaesthesia: simultaneous, multisensory perception employing two or more senses.

[2] Erwin Schrödinger (q.v.), Werner Heisenberg (uncertainty principle) C. S. Lewis: "Clive Staples Lewis" – *Chronicles of Narnia*, and Lewis Carroll, *Alice in Wonderland*.

[3] Louie Lou-eye – '60's pop song. Louie and Lou-eye are C. S. Lewis & Lewis Carroll.

[4] The sixth chakra (out of seven) is the vaunted "third eye."

[5] Agni: another term for the third eye (from the Sanskrit)

[6] Demiurge. A high official in the divine order of creating worlds. Cf. Archontes.

[7] Polyhedron/polyhedra: God, the Player, is casting 5 kinds of dice. In the 3-dimensional world of Euclid, there are only 5 that have equal sides: these are the tetrahedron (4 sides), cube (6 sides), octahedron (8 sides), dodecahedron (12)and icosahedron (20 sides). They total 50.

[8] Aether (finest medium) and quintessence (fifth element). Speculations, from the Greeks onward on the ultimate nature of reality. In modern times, the concept of the aether is invoked as an ultimate medium which permits energy – waves, particles, etc. – to travel. Among physicists it shifts in and out of favor. Quintessence was a refined medium in which memory could reside, thought could travel, etc. And much more.

[9] Sarcophagus: In the ancient Western world, sarcophagi were relief sculpted panels, often on walls or huge vases, depicting consecutive series of events – the nearest thing to moving pictures or epic TV dramas from the early Greeks to the Middle Ages.

[10] Boolean lattice: Formulated by George Boole, a 19th century Irish schoolteacher, this lattice is a sort of abstract geometrical representation of classical logic, a kind of Gordian knot. The new Alexander the Great who severed this Gordian Knot with a single stroke of his sword was yet another Irish schoolteacher from our own time, John Stewart Bell. This was the much simpler quantum lattice which removes all abstraction and goes straight for the goal, reflecting a very strange reality indeed – ours!

[11] A little humor here. *Pi* is considered to be the most irrational of all numbers (of course, it's a ratio, the circumference of the circle divided by its diameter), and ratios are the true "numbers" in nature – a very useful way of defining the concept of number in the real universe (not just counting on your fingers).

[12] Occam's Razor – from the philosopher William of Ockham (q.v.), a master of terse efficiency who hated

redundancy, and who actually said (and I translate) "entities shall not be multiplied indiscriminately." In other words, always reduce elements down to their simplest components. This, however, caused Einstein to warn: everything should be made as simple as the facts can justify, but not simpler.

[13] The anthropic principle (which even concerns the supremely aloof Stephen Hawking): the idea that no philosophy or grand unified theory can make any claim to validity unless it accounts for the fact that Man's world with all its splendors(?) was created, having ultimately spawned philosophers who speculate on the Anthropic Principle. Do you smell a fault?

[14] Carl Jung actually dreamt that this world, our world, was defecated by God, and resembles a huge turd, implying also the reason why the Creator doesn't appear to overly concern Himself with what goes on "down here." Do you smell a fault?

[15] Zippy nuts. Proponents of Zero Point Energy (ZPE) as a key to universal, boundless energy. This also brings the Higgs Boson issue to the fore. These zippy knights, led by the quixotic Sir Casimir and his sidekick, Sir Darrell Moffitt, already believe they've found the Grail, which drives the rest to distraction

[16] God, pure Spirit, is momentarily exasperated with His bride, nature, who seems to be very single-minded in her desire to reproduce endlessly. Here, He invokes, as a minced oath, one of His favorite principles: ontogeny (being) recapitulates phylogeny (origin and development of evolutionary lines in all species).

[17] Latin translation: A rigid member hath no conscience.

[18] The center of mass of the entire physical universe. Cf. three body problem

Fourth Canto

<u>The Father</u>

Time is the substance from which I am made.
Time is a river which carries me along, but I am
the river. Time is the tiger which devours me, but
I am the tiger; it is a fire that consumes me, but
I am the fire

Jorge Luis Borges

A Presence now he sensed with inner eyes,
Who seemed to speak within his deepest being.
He felt he had ascended Mount Olympus.
A voice, both gentle and insistent, played.

"Welcome home, my son. I'm very proud
Of all the pioneering that you've done
To satisfy your need for deepest truth."
The Being then embraced him inwardly.

"Within the rounded fullness of My mind,
Subsists the manifested universe,
The centers everywhere, the boundaries none,
And all the centers equitably one,
Unto which dwells your lively sentient self,
To pain and joy so prone, yet so its own,
Amazed both by its weakness and its power,
Beset and sore afflicted all around,
Whose freedoms, never absolute in nature,
Most aptly are defined in terms of limits.
These, the waypoints of My moving mind,
Create each moment of significance,
A streaming forth of new and fresh awareness.

I will vouchsafe to you a secret now.
In darkest labyrinth is born a spool of light,
Still moving on the round of nature's ocean
Within her laws, creating progeny,
Spinning forth worlds which mirror forth My own,
But freshly born, awakening to the dawn
Of *newly minted consciousness* upon
The hallowed ground of life completely new.

Its consciousness is based on *true reflection*
Of sounding light part nature and part spirit,
Which calls forth time in its reverberation.
Within the fleeting instant that it travels
Around the mirrored bubble newly blown,
It courses forth, logos like, and *in the delay*
Catches the brief reflection, *belated ray,*
Which lets My temporal consciousness be born,
Leap forth from nature's womb and fill the space--
My penetrating spirit, seed of light,
Seed unique but to itself and Me,
Prime number on the scale of the divine .
The finite born within the infinite.
A doppelganger image 'tis, brings forth
A consciousness unique within your kind:
It doubles, building image in the center,
The intersecting hub within the sphere,
Where magically, this sparking of My Mind,
Discerns itself within the concave mirror,
Orderly feels the process, senses all,
Knows itself and knows that it is knowing,
Recognizes self and calls it "I",
Builds it, builds My abode, and calls it "here,"
Within that fleeting instant calls it "now."
The clock's been set and now begins to thrum.

The god has found a home and shapes it there,
Expands a perfect sphere sensorium,
An isle, an eddy birthed within the void,
And fills it up pneumatically with spirit,
Whose swift inflation flows unchecked from Me--
Your spirit father--through your nature mother,
Whom any vacuum just cannot abide.
Each birth event contains in full the seed
Of all creation. Yet each is fully free,
Ever connected, ever tied to Me,
A true Leibnizian monadicity,[1]
Inextricably intertwined, yet free.
Here every thought expressed in every sense
In briefest time reflects the content back to center,
And since the crucible's a perfect sphere,
Then all the focal lines converge within that locus.
This junction point, this synchronizing hub,
Becomes, the moment that it gains its focus,
The bright arena of the conscious mind.

"My Will, mysterious power through which I rule,
Primary motion of the unseen God,
Emerges forth in trinitarian mind,
In cardinal, in fixed, and mutable,
Their high collectives yet inscrutable.

First, unmanifested God, creator, father
Precessing to a manifesting point, the
Second, primal logos, fixèd focus of My will;
Call it son or avatar or call it what you will,
The manifest conductor who directs
The third, My omnipresent spirit-energy,
Whose living mind subsists in mutability,
Sustaining, filling, vivifying all that is.

My motions spring from spontaneity,
From flowering forth of radiant energy.
Such creatures, of My own nobility,
Must each their destinies re-forge anew,
And catch the high effulgence of My will,
Re-living all the splendors of My mind,
Re-learning nature's structures great and small.
But ne'er must they become this nature's thrall.

Free will is a perfection, which allows
The striving spirit to experiment
With all the permutations of this mind,
But often it is too precipitate
To follow its own deep installèd path,
Its very freedom prelude to its fall,

The universe is thus, for I am wound
On Ixion's wheel, ever to make the round
Of sequent penetration and withdrawal.
Logos spermatikos[2] for its inception --
Then birth of multiplicity -- of Mine and nature's progeny;

The sequent days and nights of holy Brahmin[3]
Unfolding and infolding through eternity.
In day of manifested strife within plurality
Of nature's realm, in daylight common, for all creatures,
Followed, as night upon day, by blessed rest
Within My bosom unified, of deepest bliss unmanifest:
Eternal universe of dark and light, of dole and of delight.

Evil is not an absolute, but yet there dwell
A dark society in a shadowy hell
At three and more removes from my first rays,
In *thamasic*,[4] in self-determined gloom,
Who will not let belief take hold of them ,
Whose eyes are full averted from the light.

Spirit's thrust in nature's mystery
Has filled her nearly to capacity
Except one remnant of the cul-de-sac,
Which she, abhorring vacuum, fills herself

In any way she can. Imprisoned spirits,
This dark society entrapped within,
Are last in spirit's struggle towards perfection.
These, the willing victims of nature's jealous sway
Bring forth a being whose order is reversed–
Nature yet undirected by the spirit,
Degenerate and unregenerate.
Hard to penetrate, still harder to break,
Passive has now come active in this form.
Spirits held in bondage in this cave,
Are mired so deep they scarce can manifest--
Prisoners in darkness and in pain,
For She, desiring to possess their light,
With all her myriad powers brought to bear,
Would utterly pervert the proper balance,
In fine, created to subvert the will.

The god within forgets his mission there
Mirrors himself within the chaos deep
Within the twists and turns of nature's burl.
Yet hope remains; for through the porous gloom
The light of truth, though dimmed, still filters through;
The prisoner there need only recognize it,
And lo, the path to freedom's set before him.
'Tis there that nature's innocence,

The deep potential of her being
Remains entombed and self-corrupted,
The last to know My touch..
I cannot interfere; they're also mine.

An antimatter universe exists
Which is the mirror of your universe,
A counterpart in negative dimensions,
Which interpenetrates your world unto the core.
The one could not exist without the other;
Both would remain in stasis were there not
Asymmetry that drives the dialectic.
A tiny alteration tips the balance,
The sending forth of *logos* from My will,
A master lever activating all,
Sets carousel in motion, starts the music.

There is another structure little known
Or scarce suspected. Let me show you how
The slightest motion that your sense perceives
Can grasp upon dimensions multiplied,
Transcend its tether, see around the bend,
And come upon an insight so profound
And obvious that it will wonder why
It had not smelt it right beneath its nose.

But this I will reserve for later; now,
I must impart to you the nature of your task.

There is a deep and dread moral command,
To willful action now with which I charge you,
Newly exalted, more exposed to danger,
Not to plunge the earth, your home and mother
With all its myriad, innocent living forms
Unknowingly poised upon the precipice,
In searing pain and horrid burning death.

The die (forgive the allusion) now is cast.
To teach these things directly from the source,
I have vouchsafed this lovingly to you.
It was I who planted in your soul these seeds
Which you have deigned to nurture and to grow,
Your willed acceptance of My arduous task.
These gifts, emerged, matured, like worker ants
Bound to their queen as you are bound to Me,
Stand ready, willing, competent, to venture out.

But now I must impart to you sad news
The time's come 'round, the danger's now at hand,
Earth's to be plunged into her darkest hour.
Ignorance cannot excuse, yet now you know

And will be all the more accountable.
Look not on this as death of innocence.
The choices will be yours; free will is insurmountable.

God calls the god in you to rise, receive
Divine commission, and highest honor. I know
Your head will not be turned; you'll stay the course;
My power's more t'entreat than to command.
Your sovereign's ear you'll have for this dread task.
And so I ask, not charge, dear son, whether your will assents?"

Delaying not, the scientist looked full
Into the radiant face, the loving eyes,
Which met his own, locked on with yieldless power.
"Accept" he blurted, then he fell unconscious.
The universe at length seemed to unravel.

He woke, still on his couch; the dream was ended.
He closed both eyes again; he sought and found
A message silently inscribed therein:

"When you return to body bearing,
The images within your hearing,
The singing colors that will play
Upon your pipes a grand recital,

Airs celestial and vital,
Play a love song and a dirge,
A requiem, a symphony,
Awake the inner demiurge.
Like sheaves of grain, like ears of wheat,
Like brilliant flowers, heavenly airs
Are stored within your diadem,
And with determinate recall
Your harvest will include them all."

FOOTNOTES: FOURTH CANTO

[1] Gottfried Wilhelm von Leibniz, 17th century philosopher, bon vivant, epicure and co-inventor of the calculus (contemporaneously with Isaac Newton), believed that all of us are *monads*, unique moving points of consciousness in the universe *or* each an absolutely motionless center, depending on perspective, within whom, as in a perfect concave mirror, the entire universe plays, as in a living reflection! One of my earliest mentors, Alfred Korzybski *(General Semantics, Manhood of Humanity)* believed Leibniz to have been the most powerful intellect of the modern (post-Descartes) era.

[2] *Logos spermatikos* (Greek). The concept that before creation, God, being alone, had to do *something* to or within Himself in order to bring forth Creation. So, out of timelessness, time and multiplicity were created in a single *smooth* motion.

[3] "Days and Nights of Brahmin": As set forth here, eternally alternating periods of divine existence–day, in multiple form (that's us!), night all unified "within His bosom." The Hindus believed they alternated every 4.32 billion years (not bad, since it's 'in the range' – the same order of magnitude -- of the estimated age of the present universe – about 13 billion years).

[4] Thamasic: In early Hindu lore, one of the three states of manifested existence on the physical plane: 1) Satthwic (good), 2) Rajasic (passionate, energetic), and 3) Thamasic (self-deceived, dark, steeped in ignorance, turned away from the divine light).

The 20th century's new generation of physicists

Albert and Elsa Einstein

Einstein and other physicists at Paul Ehrenfest's home, Leyden, The Netherlsnds

Einstein with George Bernard Shaw and H. G. Wells

Einstein with wife Elsa and Charlie Chaplin

II

Time Currents
Area 51

A novel
(Excerpt)

Chapter 16: "Echoes"
Young Einstein in Zurich, 1900

Chapter 16

Echoes

<u>Zurich, Switzerland</u>   <u>January 1, 1900</u>   <u>7:25 AM</u>

Today time took its time. Precessing inexorably round the globe, starting in mid-Pacific at the International Date Line, 1900 swept Westerly an hour every 15 degrees, as the 18's clicked audibly into 19's in each time zone, coming full circle in the 24 hours. It was the first day of the 1900's, an orderly triumph of positional notation over civilization. A printer's bonanza. It was a day of fresh hope as the new century – the twentieth -- was born in number though not in numerical truth; that birth lay just a year ahead. There would be a year to savor the transition, a year in which Physics would be reborn.

In the Höttingen District of Zurich, Switzerland, Albert Einstein, a smartly dressed young man of 20 sporting a bushy new mustache, a full head of black curls and a chic fedora, strolled out into a sunny, crisp New Year's morning and strode buoyantly towards the trolley stop. It was a warm day for January, breezy, almost a harbinger of spring. Most unusual!

Regina Holstein, a comely, buxom Swiss miss, emerged from the apartment house with a black briefcase in her hand, ran after him and finally caught up with him, out of breath.

"You forgot your briefcase again, Bertie darling," she exhaled. She put her arms around his neck, smiled and kissed him sensually on the lips. They ambled to the trolley stop hand in hand and she waited with him until the brightly painted car arrived. It clanked and hummed to a stop and she kissed him again, slipping her tongue into his mouth.

"Come home soon, Bertie; I'll be waiting for you!"

He boarded the trolley, firmly grasping the steel bar with one hand, and muscled himself into the car in a single motion. It was almost empty on this New Year's morning. A group of young nurses clad in white with red cross pins and freshly starched caps sat near the front, energetically chattering away in Switzerland's quaint German dialect, Schweitzerdeutsch. It was a holiday, but the university labs knew no holiday; neither did the hospitals.

A stale alcohol smell greeted him from the seats behind him; he chose to ignore it -- New Year's Eve revelers with burgeoning hangovers dragging themelves to work.

As the huge trolley lumbered down the long hill on the wide cobblestone thoroughfare, his body and mind fell into the rhythm of the familiar clatter and rumble. He felt his body sway under the Newtonian dance, dominated by the physical forces controlling its mass and motion. But not his mind, strangely detachable from his body on this day. He could count the stones, detect their size and grouping by the short, low, occasionally shrill musical bursts, and place them into neat interacting sets, dancing geometric shapes enhanced by competing interference patterns, timing them, uniting them, conducting with his baton. Short semi-melodic passages were punctuated by the loud clang of the trolley bell, sometimes once, sometimes twice, as the lumbering iron beast periodically squeaked and groaned to a stop. If he had been blind he could have constructed a palpable moving sound picture, new sight, a substitute for sight. Music of interference patterns. Mozart must have known that; Bach surely felt it, saw it, knew it. He mouthed the words silently: I will draw the patterns with the intervals moving in an out of consonance, assign the key and play the relative frequencies on my fretless instrument! I will send it to Mahler.

Now the human voices, words only occasionally discernible, ebbed and flowed into a surreal doppler chorus, and as the trolley sped up the cobblestone chorus grew shrill in an accelerating glissando, reaching a zenith, then curving back.

The shriek and groaning of steel wheels against rails, two too-loud clangs and a hard jolt jerking his body forward and backward, snapped him out of his revery. Time to get off.

Off the steep trolley landing he stepped, onto the slippery cobblestones. Down the hill he looked long and hard. Swimming into his view, shores of the Zűrichsee glistened at the bottom, 100 meters below, waves played palpably on the shore. His peripheral vision merged into an intense wide angle view, everything in a single dance, a peculiar order. Fleeting shafts of sunlight punctuated the moving landscape with strobe-like rhythmic glints off the waves.

Up rose a stiff gust, nearly blowing his hat off. The spell broken, he sniffed, inhaled and composed himself. Hand on hat, he briskly strode eastward toward the grey, austere building that held the physics labs.

He mounted two flights of stairs and walked into his shared office, sat in his chair and put his feet up on the desk. The phone jingled. It was his office-mate Heinrich, an older fellow student; his wife was about to deliver, so he wouldn't be coming in today. To be sure!

Endeavoring to regain his focus, he removed some papers from his briefcase, Some of Poincaré's latest work. He already knew many of the equations by heart; more were forthcoming. He could write them on the slate within his brain, but today they were strange hieroglyphs; within them lurked a mystery. They pulsed, they danced.

Suddenly something lit up, glowed bright green in his brain; an image of streams of brilliant light flowing into one. He lapsed briefly into unconsciousness, then snapped awake, disturbed at losing control of his mind even for an instant. He looked up at the clock on the mantlepiece; its bell sounded, three sets of three. It was exactly 9 A.M.

Threeness! Three majestic chords in E_b, major, three flats, *portamento,* echoing the number 3, three triumphant major chords ending the opening movement of Beethoven's Eroica, the third, breaking forever free from Papa Haydn, free to burn his own shining track into the earth. The music played in his mind, dictated the time, saturating spaces of time, times of space, infinitely expandable, compressible, in inverse proportion. He fastened his mind to the rhythm, partially dissociating to observer within observer who took snapshots in the rhythm -- elastic trajectories at zenith and nadir conversely crisscrossing, expanding and compressing. His perspective foreshortened to a disappearing point and instantaneously dilated to infinity in a timeless still-point moment, now reversing, time resuming. Ever discernible times of space, spaces of time, space peculiarly curved, the curve ever palpable. He could feel its arc; he traveled on the light beam, upon its arc.

He was momentarily disoriented. A sudden insight like a bursting sunrise appeared on the inner horizon of his concentric consciousness, rising, quickly illuminating the entire sphere. He strove to rivet his focus on it, drawing it into the light as it dawned on him, reviewing, replaying. He tightly focused the ray of his mind's eye upon the outer layer of the sphere, outer reaches of its tether, a concave mirror, in novel ways reflecting, amplifying, revealing all that emanated from within in a language of flashes, glints and shafts; new in-sights. Alive and active; it was a newly functioning part of him. He listened with inner gaze.

Deeply embedded in those hieroglyphs lurked a mystery; suddenly he saw patterns in them, patterns of jade light; parts of the equations seemed to rise off the page and glow; they played; the flat printed page two-dimensional grew a third axis and then shimmered on a fourth, a moving axis. alternating, merging and remerging from the infinite to the infinitesimal, maxima and minima. Minkowski, my dearest teacher, are you with me?

Re-replaying the journey, he focused anew on the hieroglyphs, concentrating harder than he had ever done. The secret was in the curves and in the interference patterns. Time *and* space? *Time-space?!!* An epiphany. Could it be? He concentrated long and hard on the thought, scribbling furiously, hiding his papers under other papers whenever someone entered the room. There it was, waiting for him all the time. *Zero sum*, a dance, a *coincidentia oppositorum*. Why couldn't Poincaré see it? He *must* have seen it; could he ignore it?

His heart pounded, his shallow breathing punctuated by powerful cadences that shook his frame. What time is it? Indeed!

Several students and assistants had entered the electrical lab in the next room. He hadn't noticed until now. Minkowski was in Bern for the holiday; he wouldn't return until next Thursday.

Einstein's fellow students passed like moving shadows back and forth before the open office door; caricatures of themselves; their voices a dull cacaphony; sounds blurred, the occasional pop and sizzle of the electrical devices. Nobody greeted him; he was alone in a small crowd. His center of consciousness hovered at the edge, the breach in his mirrored sensorium, the inside of the reflective sphere where time-space had intruded. Simple question. He looked out his office window at the huge clock on the grey monolith of a bank building; the minute hands moved visibly; he could feel the crawl of the hour hands.

He gave a start. It was a quarter of eleven. Where had two hours gone? Putting both hands down on his desk he bent forward until his forehead touched the cool desk. It's all right, he thought; this is all new; this is a breakthrough. He sat up as awareness grew of the depth and intensity of this insight. Bubbles of light pulsed upward into his back brain as elation grew -- a broad smile emanating from the depths; his whole being smiled.

Suddenly he realized he was hungry. Grabbing his notes, he quickly descended the narrow stone stairway, inhaled the bracing air, and then briskly walked nine blocks to the Pantheon, a well known Greek restaurant in downtown Zurich. He was early; only a few tables were occupied.

Sophia, the owner's daughter, a slim, sultry lass who liked his trim good looks and his penetrating eyes, gave him the menu and lingered, trying to catch his eye. Too preoccupied to flirt with her today, he ordered his usual lunch--a bowl of hot soup and a lamb *souvlaki*. Barely acknowledging Sophia as she decorously set his food in front of him, he ate quickly, slurping the soup, pushed the plate aside, and resumed his intent concentration.

Scarcely aware of the passage of two entire hours, he remained in the mahogany booth, filling an entire notebook with arcane mathematical symbols. The owner, George Theophanopoulos, became annoyed; he was monopolizing the booth for too long. He stood before the booth, arms akimbo, but before he could utter a word, Einstein glared at him angrily with luminous green eyes. Theophanopoulous retreated in terror muttering Greek imprecations, performing an elaborate Orthodox sign of the cross.

When he returned, in a virtual trance, he had the lab office to himself. He worked most of the afternoon, and at about 4:45, heard a clamor in the next room where several men were crowding around the wire, chattering excitedly.

III

Voyage of the Opal

Journey of the twinned photon
a frolic

Voyage of the Opal

I. Journey to Andromeda

Setting out to span the world,
Beginning in the singlet state,
A humble photon androgyne,
Janus faced[1], did train its gaze,
Twinned in diametric phase,
In antithetical directions,
Launched upon the sea of spacetime
In its crystal maiden voyage.

The little photon humbly sought
Its *stitch in time* which shapes our ends;
An eye of God, the oldest god,
From pantheon of antiquity,
From time stepped into timelessness.
First in all, yet god of endings,
'Twas Janus[1] guardian of the portals,
Alpha, omega, friend of mortals,
(Mick and Nick in Finnegan's Wake)[2]
In his bifurcating state,

A perfect monadicity,
An epsilon of consciousness--
Unbroken mode of consciousness--
Unlimited by space and time,
Twinnable within its nature,
It stayed within the unit mode,
Full cognizant of its collective.

While human minds believe he flew
Across the vast expanses free,
A living crystal beckoned he
While eons passed in human time.

The ancient god now squared himself,
Looking out in *four* directions
This *Brahmin*[3] particle's name was Vision.
He exponentiated further,
Now Nature viewed in all directions,
Implicate in all dimensions,
Explicate in all declensions,
Omnipresent, omnitemporal
Paradigm of frequencies.
All the overtones, harmonics,
Vibratory pentatonics,

Perfect fifths and rising tonics,
Exponents' acceleration,
Manifest in powers of one.[4]

With fractal infinite variation,
And all dimensions' resolution
In a rhythmic absolution,
This ultimate superconductor
Unified it all in ductance.
Unit of divine awareness
Storming Nature's dense reluctance
Coupled with her coy acceptance
(Rather like approach-avoidance),
Descried the crystal in his glass;
Persisted, *made the stitch in time.*
As eons folded round a point,
They disappeared and time collapsed;
All intervening history lapsed.

Out in Andromeda, our twin,
Within a spiral arm extern
Where Surya's[5] counterpart did burn,
A million light years traveled he.
A picosecond after tierce,[6]
A calcite crystal he did pierce.

At once he switched polarity.
An *instant* switch from he to she,
And in the selfsame point in time
(Proportionate to space inversely)
A full *two* million light years hence,
To demonstrate androgyny,
Instantaneously,
The other end became a she!
We called it *action-at-a-distance*--
Professor Bell's A A A D.[7]

Creator smiled inscrutably.

For photon twin, 'twas unity
Within its being out of time
To stretch itself through vasty space
And tower through eleven dimensions,
All those light years notwithstanding,
To complicate its ten extensions.
The beast was just androgynary
Whose motions made a single binary;
And if you think that's oxymoron
Look in the nucleus of Boron
Or better yet Beryllium,
Or the strange mind of Terry Gilliam.

So sacrifice your common sense
Upon the non-discursive altar
Of grand hypotheses provisional;
Sail West beyond the ribbed Gibraltar
Of circumscribed ratiocination.

Logos spermatikos[8] they called it
Or just a holy masturbation;
Can it be a quantum lattice
Within a chain of fornication?
The photon world may be the key,
For logos was a photon twin--
Yet a singularity–
Unit *and* collective of
Divine awareness and perception--
The bridge 'twixt time and timelessness
Looking back at his creator,
Looking forward into Nature,
Joining unit and collective
Mystically in a dyad.[9]

All the rest are its descendants,
Flames within the parent flame;
All revert to singular
Living in their collective phase;

All disperse in deepest nature,
To the monad, at each point
Along space-time's continuum.

So, sequent time he did unravel.
The particle was always one,
With and within the singularity
Where no duration does subsist,
But buried deep in Nature's realm
Undriven by the timebound spheres
Its singularity exists
Throughout *en*foldings of dimensions
*Un*foldings, tensions and extensions.
And Universe did interact
Entwining 'round this marv'lous blip
While he appeared to make the trip;
He wasn't going anywhere,
Much like Frank Herbert folding space,
More like Tim Leary folding time.

How to resolve this weird conundrum
Within a universe so humdrum:
If folding space could conquer time,
Then folding time should run apace
Within proportions full reversed--

A unified organic moment.
The causal chains in each event
Departed and arrived at once.

.

II. Relativity Revisited

Now how's that possible, you may ask,
When all our science teachers swear:
For any sub-light vehicle
Attaining Albert Einstein's limit,
The transformations of Lorentz
Would shrink it to a tiny trice
While mass approached infinity.

Although it only has two terms—
Tied arbitrarily together,
Traveler accelerating out,
Observer supposedly at rest,
Given a *privileged* seat to test
(Although we know he's moving, too),
Extrapolate from that position,
And you, *Smith,* soon will ask just why
Old *Jones,* the pilot of that craft
Accelerating off so fast,
Wouldn't be thinking the same thing—
That *you* were nearing light speed-*c,*
And gaining mightily in weight.
Add to that each point in spacetime

Strung along continuous worldlines,
Inextricably intertwined.
So the conclusion's inescapable
If Einstein's were correct surmises:
We can only run in circles,
Or vortices, to tell the truth;
Each is relative to the other,
And one man's rest's the other's flight
Accelerating away from him,
In the curving of the cone
(*A term for spiral well-inscribed*
In plenum's[10] *edgeless boundaries*).

Meanwhile, Jones, flying alone
On steady power, uniform
Acceleration at one G,[11]
Anticipated great resistance
As his ship began approaching
The unattainable speed of light.
Amazement crossed his features when
His clocks and instruments didn't slow,
But passed the magic barrier, "*c*"
And sped on steadily, predictably:
Two *c*, three *c*, four *c*, eight –
No hyperspace or mystic state!

At rest the mass cannot be felt.
Even old Jones, shrunk to a point,
Who weights ten trillion trillion tons
Thinks *he's* in a state of rest
And marvels at *your* size and weight,
Thinks you, Smith, should be on a diet.
And what of all the other monads
Holding each his state of rest,
With absolute, unique relation
In each and every permutation
To each and every other monad
Swimming in the sea of spacetime,
That paradigm of merging cones?

It's certainly obvious to me
That we've relation to them, too,
Each and every tiny trice
And massive juggernaut in space:
Unless I am a mental slattern
I'm starting to perceive a pattern:
Sum them over and you'll see
This universe's curvature
(for doubtless there are many others)
If finite but unbounded be,
Or else a bound infinity

(Behold the new antinomy),
As plenum unified, it lives;
It might be simpler than you think.

Now:
There's something fishy 'bout all this;
I'm guessing that you smell it, too!
Einstein's keen scent detected it,
And Einstein was a Pisces, true!
If all are in a state of rest,
And yet accelerating, too,
The secret has to lie within
The ligatures within the swirl
That make a moving master pattern,
Permutations infinite,
Coherent elasticity
In lines of force that are writ large
Upon the tablature of life;
Divinity that shapes our process,
Endless streams of living force,
Monads strung like pearls upon
The complex necklace of existence;
Grand collective hierarchies
Of phase, of frequency, of mass,
Phases in continuum.

We've all been told size doesn't matter;
How much you weigh? That's up to you!
But let's get serious once again:
Think of the event horizon
Of your biggest, blackest hole;
Super galactic dynamo;
Gravitation strong enough
To bend the light waves round the curve.
Remember Einstein's well-took labors
Tied gravity to acceleration.
If photons fly at one speed– c --
Within a vacuum here or there,
They must have traveled far and wide
Within the purview of the hole,
Distances seemingly compressed
But unaffected in contraction,
Infinity in the palm of the hand,
Eternity within an hour.

Think of it as an ice cream cone,
Which narrows to a perfect point,
Then widening on the other side
Continuing on to double cone,
A folding in of time in space.
A folding out of space in time

Through which all passes ineluctably,
Compressing to infinite density
Into primordial substance, *ylem*
Upon the vertex of that cone,
Gnab gib, zero point, big bang–
Energies of such intensity
Re-forming, on emergence
Into a new created universe --
Convergence of infinities,
Emerging on the other side
Expanding in the widening cone.

Our Cygnus X, within the Swan,
The black hole in our neighborhood,
A mere ten thousand light years hence,
At nearby edge of vaunted light-cone
Sitting right in our backyard,
Suggests the cones are not so far
Away in normal world-lines,
But sit among us, multiplying,
Merging into primal patterns,
In a plenum paradigm.

Remember Jones, so far away,
Accelerating past the limit?
Now think of *Brown*, another pilgrim,
Sitting in the *Beagle* ship,
Passing the sprinkles on the cone
Approaching the event horizon
Of our near neighbor, Cygnus X.
He disappears, we mourn his loss,
Certain he's been stretched to floss.
But Brown, who's looking back at us,
Transported to a newer time,
May see *his* former home a new
Event horizon as he courses.

Think next of photon's single speed.
If the photon's speed is constant
And it's "trapped" within that hole,
Nearest border of the cone,
Distances there cannot be else that
Astronomical in breadth:
A baby universe perhaps,
Forever sundered from our own.

III. Boundless Inscape

I, too, have curiosity
To learn where all that energy,
That shrinking breadth and burgeoned mass
Is coming from. It has to rise
From points upon the world lines
Whereon we ride, *our* Ixion's wheel.
The quantum world, the microcosm.
Underlies the macrocosm,
Underpins it, permeates it.

All's in the mind, it seems to me,
But whose mind? Your mind? Mine? His? God's?
As if the outreach of the monad,
Beknottedness of Spirit's gonad,
Subsists in curve parameters,
Within a certain limitation:
Centripetal degree of arc
In sinister chirality,
In downward exponentiation.
Steepening through many rounds,
Each octave for each curving in
Relating to each outer octave

In full related subtleties,
To *zero point*, where energies
Of inexhaustible supply
Re-innervate the living curves.
The adversary of Hercules,
Antaeus, found his strength renewed
Each time his foot did touch its ground.

These structures pre-exist, it's true,
But in dimensionality,
(Remember that it's in *your* court);
Those energies are yours and mine,
Each to his own, and fully felt,
And in dimensional orientation
Such as we live in, in this world.
We travel ever up and down
These exponentiated gyres,
And feel the living energies,
Exult or suffer in their fires.

Now to the *right* spirality,
In fanning out unto the limit
Of gentlest curve, the highest octave.
For there the boulevard meanders
Beyond the borders of ourselves

And joins the monads next to us.
One wonders if our vaunted *pi*
Is just a fraction off exactness
So that we are not bound in circles,
Strict in their diameters,
But spirals, vortices instead,
Closely sharing frequencies,
Within the light cone that we share.

It seems with each dimension shift
Affecting actual curvature
Exists a true conversion factor
Easy to approximate.
Where left spirality goes out
And right spirality turns in:
This *tetrad,* fourfold totality,
Sums up the possibilities
Of spiral/vortex in the cones --
Those interpenetrating gyres --
Where time and curvature are bound,
And, yes, there *is* a difference.

Now some are arcing out of reach
Just like our friend the traveler,
Much like ourselves from *his* purview,

While doubtless others are arriving
As their curl unbends to ours,
Wavefronts coming into phase
Upon our range of curvature.
For transformations of Lorentz,
Clearly cannot be other than
Reference points, all relative,
For me, for you, for everyone.
Sum them over and you'll know.

IV. The Matrix

But that's sub-light; there is another
Side to this called F T L;[12]
Here, the particles cannot slow down
All the way to light speed–*c*,
Unless they've infinite nether mass,
And well reversèd ā-Lorentz.[13]
Their version of our vaunted rest
Is infinite velocity, no jest!
And if you'll stop to analyze it,
It means they're everywhere at once.
But when they start their slowing down
To-wards the crawl of lightspeed–*c*,
It's *back-in-time* that they are moving,
As sub-light moves ahead in time.

Image it and you'll see a swirl
Around a point between the two—
The still point of that turning world,
The locus of the present—now.

But what's between, you may well ask.
To understand, turn it around and
Study Michelson's and Morley's
Proof that ordinary motion
Won't affect the seeming speed that
Photon waves appear to travel.
Right there's a hint; they're not affected
By speeds so relative down here.

Imagine now a special matrix,
A matrix of unique potential,
World of light connected to us,
True in singularity,
Living within its own dimensions,
Affecting us but not affected.
Infinitely sensitive,
Joining every spacetime point,
There already, it only waits
Upon the generating signal
Manifesting from our action,
In measured portion, while the rest,
Inseparably from the whole,
Lurks within the matrix, quite
Attuned to all our willed commands
Or Nature's purposed operations:

Stable as Gibraltar's rock,
Standing quite outside of time,
Surrounding us dimensionally,
Within, without, and ever touching.

Macroscopic quantum world,
It's mystically always ready
To show its *partiality*,
A timeless realm where photons bask
In photon singularity.

The still point of the turning world,
Primal Omphalos[14]*, grand redactor,*
Spirit of the Great Attractor,[15]
Home of endless pure potential,
Source of all infinities,
Of archetype and pure idea.

What's that you say, my brother Albert,
There really isn't such a thing?
More's happening within this world
Than dreamt in your philosophy.
A Scotus *implicatio--* [16]
Erigena, not John the Dunce [17]-
A Cusan *explicatio* [18]

In pseudo-Dionysian[19]
Ana-logic, ana-kata.
Laws of the excluded middle,
Identity, non-contradiction,[20]
Now were playing second fiddle,
For if we had just *both* and *neither*
And lots of play in all dimensions
Universe could have a breather
And find relief for all her tensions.

Aristotle's formularies,
Taken all too seriously,
By all accounts, deleriously
In the thirteenth century,
When Aquinas got commissioned
For the Summa Theologic.
Old Aristotle's new hodge-podgic
Freshly tailored for the Pope,
Divided paths of faith *and* reason:
Dual choices for salvation
For each and every *peregrin*
Who would become a *comprehensor.*

Creator frowned inscrutably.

It was as if the great attractor
Locus of the grand redactor
Shaped its ends despite rough-hewing,
Making everything worth doing.
Interstice insinuation
Wound around about the nation
In and out and *ana-kata*
Hearkening the roof-brain chatter,
Littered with the strange attractors.

But every single world line
Did merge with each and every other
Mother, brother, pother, t'other
In all potential gradients
And all shone with a radiance
As each proclaimed the other brother,
Son and daughter, father, mother,
Consort each to every other.
Order did unfold at random,
Singularities in tandem,
Hundredth monkey notwithstanding.

"We're utterly impenitent,
For what should nobler venue gain,"
God lamented once again,
"If We should seal Our hard consent
And patch you straight into the collective,
Rewire Albert's right-hand brain,
As mathematical detective,
As if the universe, Our brain
Could not assert Its fiery will
Ubiquitously all at once!
The arrogance of John the Dunce[21]
Would bind me up in logic shackles,
The while he spouts divine invectives.

A humble Irishman named Bell
Will soon be harrowing this hell."

FOOTNOTES: *VOYAGE OF THE OPAL*

[1] *Janus*, a twin-faced Greek god of portals and of beginnings and endings, the earliest god in the Greek pantheon.

[2] *Finnegan's Wake* (James Joyce): "The ballad of Mick and Nick." Cf. Nicholas of Cusa's *coincidentia oppositorum*, a dance of contraries

[3] Brahma, the supreme HIndu god, was represented with faces turned in 4 directions, symbolizing his omniscience.

[4] Although 1 to any power, in our present understanding of exponents is 1, the two roots --square root of 1 (1^2) are 1 and -1. The square root of -1 is i, the "imaginary number," making it a 4th root of 1. For some reason, popular mathematics takes it no further, refusing to speculate on the square root of $-i$, whose square root would be j, an 8th root of 1. And so on *ad infinitum*. Not a convenient axiom for basic mathematics, thus, largely ignored.

It is my instinctive believe that both the negative and positive powers of 1 have antecedents – referents – in reality, virtual realities, mental or imaginary realities, black holes and white holes, etc. Here may be buried the Holy Grail of physics – the secret of quantum gravity.

⁵ *Surya*: Sanskrit for the sun

⁶ *Tierce*: In Chaucer's age, the third canonical hour: 9 AM. *Picosecond*: 1/1,000,000,000,000 second (trillionth)

⁷ A.A.A.D: action at a distance

⁸ *Logos spermatikos*: A theory of original creation in which God created Himself, signifying birth of the Logos, through which the manifested world was then created. The unmanifest God had to do something with Himself. Other theories suggest the He, seed of Spirit, interacted with Her, ground of Nature, the moment in which history began, the birth of space and time, i.e., spacetime. In modern terms, the Big Bang.

⁹ Dyad: defined as "two units regarded as one." A mystical numerological concept of 2-in-1. Compare the Christian concepts of Trinity, 3-in-1. Numerology necessarily plays a crucial (pun unintended) role in all myths/theories of creation.

¹⁰ *Plenum*, also called *pleroma*. The totality of the filled universe containing everything – all that is – whether it be conceived of as *finite but unbounded* or a *bounded infinity*. I call it "boundless inscape."

¹¹ One G: equivalent to normal gravity on earth, where his weight would feel normal. Accelerating to two G he would feel double his weight, and so on.

¹² FTL: faster than light

[13] ā-Lorentz: reversal of the Lorentz transformation, based on 4 dimensional Minkowski space, which simply adds a time axis -- a fourth coordinate added to the normal three (right-left, forward-backward, up-down). Because of our orientation within three dimensional space, we perceive the fourth, time, as moving. Since each higher dimension totally subsumes the next lower one. In n spatial dimensions, four, five or more, the time dimension would be $n+1$.

[14] *Omphalos*: An ancient Greek concept of the world's navel

[15] Great attractor "GA": A special point within universe -- "all that is" -- the true center of all mass in the universe, traceable in an unbroken timeline from Big Bang to the present. From our perspective it's moving, *precessing*; but from GA's. the universe not only revolves around it (as it does in all perspectives) but is "seen" from the viewpoint of the original expanding center.

[16] Johannes *Scotus* Erigena: 9th century Irish neoplatonic philosopher. *Implicatio*: infolding, along with *explicatio,* unfolding, creating the Neoplatonic rhythm.

[17] A warning not to confuse Erigena (9th century neoplatonist) with Duns Scotus (14th century), a scholastic who out Aquinased Aquinas. Their philosophies were diametrically opposed.

[18] Nicholas Cusanus (Cardinal Nicholas of Cusa), 15th century neoplatonic philosopher, far ahead of his time in philosophy and in mathematics.

[19] 5th-6th century neoplatonic philosopher, whose writings were first erroneously thought to be those of the biblical Dionysius the Aeropagite.

[20] Laws of identity, non-contradiction and the excluded middle: the foundation of Aristotle's logic

[21] John Duns Scotus, 1266-1308. "Doctor Subtilis", wily Scotsman, hyper-scholastic Franciscan monk who out-Aquinased Aquinas.

ABOUT THE AUTHOR

Dr. Frederic deJavanne (An De Zhe), is a gifted author, linguist (six modern languages, three ancient languages), translator and editor – and musician. He has served as professor, vice-chancellor and college president at three major Chinese universities: Tsinghua University, Harbin Medical University, and Harbin University of Commerce. He fell in love with science at age 14, and for many years, "loved science more than any woman."

His wide-ranging interests, besides quantum physics and mathematics, include metaphysics, ancient and medieval cosmology, astronomy, James Joyce, Greek and Chinese philosophy, and psycholinguistics.

His books include, among others, *Word Power*—a textbook and teaching encyclopedia of English word origins for university students, written in English and Chinese; two novels -- *Time Currents* and *Beware the Fury*; *Waterlogged Chopstix* (an irreverent guide for foreign residents of China); *The Comic Apocalypse*—a study of and guide to James Joyce's *Ulysses*; and original translations, French into English, of *Vertigo of the Void* and *Being and Time* by French philosopher Eugene de Grandry, for which he was awarded the coveted *Grand Prix Humanitaire de France*.

Prof. deJavanne served as Senior Editor *of International Review of the Arts,* and Associate Editor of *Heartland Magazine* and *The Inkslinger's Review.* A pianist and composer as well, he has two music CD's to his credit: "Live at the Palace" and "The Phantom of the Piano."

He has four grown children who have so far produced seven grandchildren including two sets of twins. Residing in Harbin, China (next door to Siberia), he winters gratefully each year at his other home in Phoenix, Arizona.